PROTECTED BY THE ALIEN WARRIOR

HOPE HART

The Arcav Alien Invasion Series

The Arcav King's Mate

The Arcav Commander's Human

The Arcav General's Woman

The Arcav Prince's Captive

A Very Arcav Christmas

The Arcav Captain's Queen

The Arcav Guard's Female

The Warriors of Agron Series

Taken by the Alien Warrior

Claimed by the Alien Warrior

Saved by the Alien Warrior

Seduced by the Alien Warrior

Protected by the Alien Warrior

Captured by the Alien Warrior

Rescued by the Alien Warrior

Enticed by the Alien Warrior

CHAPTER ONE

I^{vy}

The Voildi dumps me on the ground, and I glower up at him.

This planet is kicking my ass.

"Get up," he says as he steps forward. He raises his hand while Zoey slowly gets to her knees, her face so pale she looks half dead.

The asshole is going to hit her.

I jump in front of Zoey, and Beth helps her to her feet.

The Voildi are a sickly yellow color, with sharp, pointed teeth. They're about our height, but they're stronger than most of the firefighters I work with, and they're some of the strongest people around.

After the way the Voildi kicked my ass when we were taken, I'm prepared for his speed. He swings, and I automatically duck, punching him in the face. The thud of my fist is satisfying as he cups his hands to his nose, and his friends roar with laughter as blood drips between his fingers.

The gag in my mouth makes it difficult to breathe. Thanks to the time I broke my nose when I was ten, I'm limited by the amount of oxygen I can get through it. I raise my fists as he steps forward anyway, more than ready for a fight.

"Jasit," a voice says, and we all turn. I've seen a few sociopaths in my time, but one glance at this guy has all the tiny hairs on the back of my neck standing up. He glances at me, and I shiver as I raise my chin.

His gaze shifts, lingering on Zoey and Beth, and he frowns. "Where are the rest?"

"The Braxians showed up," Jasit grinds out. "They killed the hunters from Atar's pack."

The other Voildi nods, and from the tension in the Voildi surrounding us, I'm guessing he's the ringmaster of this little circus.

"Are you sure we can't eat them?" Jasit asks, and his leader smiles.

"I have plans for them," he says. "Meat can be found anywhere on this planet. But females are a precious commodity."

Oh, great.

The leader raises his eyebrow, gesturing to the right, and I tense at the sight of the cave entrance.

"Walk," he says.

We walk. I glance at Beth, and she nods, making sure Zoey is between us. The cave is larger than it first appeared, lit with torches that have been attached to the walls. Someone is cooking meat, and my stomach growls.

Cannibals, Ivy. You probably don't want what they're cooking.

There's a fire burning, and a group of Voildi are gathered around it—women and children included.

One of the Voildi unties my gag, and I run my dry tongue against the corners of my mouth. The leader offers Beth a waterskin, and she hesitates, stepping back as he smiles at her.

"We want you alive," he says through that creepy-ass smile. "So drink, or we will pour it down your throat."

She takes a sip, and I gratefully do the same when I'm handed a skin of my own.

We're pointed toward a corner on the opposite side of the fire, and I snort at the thin furs as I glance around. Beth's eyes meet mine, and I nod. Yeah, we're unlikely to be able to sneak out of here anytime soon.

One of the Voildi women steps forward, avoiding my gaze. She hands us each a plate of food, and we sit down. But we're not in a hurry to sample whatever these guys are serving us.

I inspect it and finally shrug as Zoey and Beth watch me. Looks like I'm taking one for the team.

I take a bite and swallow with a relieved sigh. "It's fish," I tell them, and we inhale our food as the Voildi finish their own meals, breaking into groups as they pass around thick furs.

Zoey hands me her plate, and I run my eyes over her. She looks bad, her skin so pale that her blue eyes provide the only color on her face. I lock eyes with Beth and nod. We need to find someone who can help her.

When we were stolen from Earth and sold to the aliens who loaded us onto their ship, one of those motherfuckers kicked Zoey in the ribs. Before we were taken by the Voildi, I'd had a quick look at the damage. If I'd come across her while in the field, I'd have taken her straight to the hospital.

I'm not a doctor, but after six years as a firefighter, I've seen it all. And I'd bet money that she has at least one fractured rib.

The urge for vengeance hits me, soothed only by the fact that those purple assholes died when we crash-landed on this planet.

Just when we thought we'd been rescued, the three of us were separated from the other human women.

I finger what's left of my Minnie Mouse pajamas. The pajamas were a gag gift from Bruce, my closest friend and fellow firefighter. The huge black man roared with laughter when I waltzed into the communal kitchen at our firehouse wearing the bright-pink pajamas.

I spent our entire journey to this cave ripping scraps of material from my pajamas and hiding them along the way. I'm pinning all my hopes on the other women coming after us—ideally with the huge warriors who stepped in to fight off the first group of Voildi who tricked us into following them.

I scan our surroundings, but nothing has changed since I did the same thing a few minutes ago. The floor is bumpy with tree roots, and there's a small puddle of water not far from where I'm sitting, growing larger with the occasional drop of water from somewhere above us.

Time to figure out a plan.

"We're not getting out of here tonight," I murmur to the other women. "But that's okay. We're not in good condition, and we need to sleep anyway."

Beth nods. "If they've got plans, they might move us."

"Or they could bring those plans to us," Zoey murmurs.

I shake my head. "This looks temporary. Look—those guys are arguing over blankets, and it's clear that this camp has been set up in a hurry."

Beth shifts next to me. "So what do we do?"

I sigh, annoyed at myself. I've had to wrestle with my temper my whole life, and I mentally curse my poor impulse control.

"I was a dumbass and showed them I could fight. Now they're going to watch me closely. They know Zoey's injured, and they've already discounted you as a thin weakling," I say to Beth, rolling my eyes.

I went to high school with a ballet dancer, and she could give any firefighter a run for their money when it came to mental and physical toughness.

I wait as one of the Voildi comes close to our corner of the cave and then lower my voice to a whisper.

"We need to be realistic," I say. "We're outnumbered. By a lot. Chances are, we're not all making it out of here together."

A sob escapes Zoey's throat, and for a moment I feel bad about my bluntness. But if we're going to come up with a plan, we all need to get on the same page, and fast.

Beth grabs Zoey's hand and stares at me. "We can't split up," she says.

I squint my eyes at her. "We do whatever is best for all of us. If even one of us can escape, we can get help for the others."

Beth glances away, and I drop it. For now. We huddle together as the temperature falls, not bothering to talk as the Voildi all go to sleep.

I watch for any opportunity for us to sneak out of here, but there must be twenty Voildi between us and the cave entrance, not to mention the sentries outside. I get a few hours of sleep as Beth takes over the watch, but by the time the Voildi start putting out their fire, I'm so tired I feel nauseous.

One of the Voildi steps forward, handing me a waterskin. I pass it to Zoey, and Beth gently encourages her to take a few sips before Zoey pushes it away and we share the rest amongst us.

A few moments later, a Voildi makes the mistake of coming too close, and Beth thrusts out one of her long, toned legs. The Voildi trips, and we all chortle as he face-plants.

"Whoops." Beth grins as he bares his teeth at us. "My bad."

The leader approaches, and I stare at him as he narrows his eyes at Beth.

"We may want you alive, but that doesn't mean you need to be healthy," he murmurs, and the threat is scarier for the controlled rage in his voice.

"It was an accident," Beth says sweetly, and I hold back a grin. "I needed to stretch."

He turns away and gestures to one of the other Voildi.

"Get up," that Voildi says.

We help Zoey to her feet and follow him out of the cave. I inhale the fresh air, grateful that we managed to make it through another night on this terrifying planet. What I'd give to wake up in the firehouse right now. I'd love to discover that this was all just a bad dream.

Suck it up, Ivy. Get moving.

"I need the bathroom," I announce, and the Voildi next to us obviously have no idea what I'm talking about. I sigh. "I need to piss." I cross my legs and do the universal pee bounce until one of them snorts.

"Killis?" the Voildi calls, and the leader moves toward us. How nice to put a name to his face. They have a short discussion, and Killis finally shoots me a warning look, pointing to three Voildi, who lead me into the forest.

This is not good.

"I can't go with you looking at me." I scowl at them. Two of them turn away, but one shrugs, his eyes cold as he gestures for me to do my business. Once again, I curse my impulsiveness. I shrug and drop my pajamas, getting on with it under his watchful eye.

No opportunities to escape for me.

They lead me back to the group, and I shake my head at Beth. Her face falls, and I can practically read her mind. She's realizing that since I'm too closely watched, she's going to have to be the one to escape.

We walk for hours, surrounded by Voildi. Eventually, I shoot Beth a look.

"I can't," she mutters.

"You have to. You're our only hope."

I don't want to be a bully, but I will if I need to. Zoey collapsed a few minutes ago, and she's currently being carried by one of the Voildi, who doesn't look pleased.

Beth frowns, her expression dejected. "I'm not really the hero type," she mutters. "I'm more decorative."

I grin at that. "Buck up, champ. You're on."

Beth sighs, sways, and drops down to her knees. One of the Voildi orders her to get up, his leg cocked threateningly. She gets back up to her feet, and I glower at the Voildi.

"Takes a big man to kick someone while they're down," I mutter.

Then Beth trips, hitting the ground, and one of the Voildi picks her up, throwing her over his shoulder. She glances at me, not pleased, but I can see the acceptance on her face. She needs to look weak if this is going to work. The Voildi are likely to see her thin body and assume she's no threat at all, completely ignoring the toned muscles that speak of hours of training every day.

Idiots.

"I need to pee," she says finally, and her face is white with fear as she meets my gaze one more time while the Voildi carrying her mutters something to his friends.

I nod at her. Right now, she's our only hope.

Ivy

Killis is incoherent with rage when Beth doesn't come back. It took a while for everyone to notice that the Voildi sent to guard Beth hadn't returned with her, and a group of Voildi were dispatched to go back for them.

They've now returned with their friend slumped over one of the Voildi's shoulders, the vicious wound on his head dripping blood onto the forest floor. It's taking every ounce of my willpower to not do a victory dance.

Nice work, Beth.

After a few moments of watching Killis scream at his men, spittle flying from his mouth, I tune him out. The translation device in my ear is the only thing that allows me to understand him anyway. Instead, I watch his men as he chews them out, calling them various names as his yellow face darkens until it's the color of Dijon mustard.

A few of his men look suitably contrite. But the Voildi closest to me protests as Killis orders them to leave their injured friend in the forest.

Killis doesn't give a shit.

"Let this be a lesson to all of you," he hisses. His men comply, placing the injured Voildi on the ground, but a few of them hesitate.

Dissension in the ranks. Awesome.

My dad was a firefighter—a lieutenant in the FDNY. He was loved by the firefighters in his company, and I wanted to be just like him when I grew up.

When he was home, Dad often talked about his favorite book—*The Art of War*.

Sometimes, he'd read me parts before I fell asleep. Most of it I didn't understand until I read it again when I was an adult. One of the quotes he loved the most: *"Treat your men as you would your own beloved sons. And they will follow you into the deepest valley."*

My dad was known for this. He'd never ask anyone in his company to do something he wasn't willing to do himself.

From the look on the Voildi's faces, they're not feeling like Killis's beloved sons.

But they still leave their friend behind.

Zoey is either unconscious or smart enough to pretend that she's unconscious, which leaves me as the target of Killis's fury.

I expect things to get worse for me, and they do. Killis has my hands tied again and then slaps me across the face, screaming at me in front of his men. I stare back at him silently, keeping my face blank.

Eventually, I realize he sees my gaze as a challenge, and I drop my eyes to the ground, hunching my shoulders.

"If your opponent is of choleric temper, seek to irritate him. Pretend to be weak, that he may grow arrogant."

I'll make him pay for everything he's done to us.

We walk all day and only stop to make camp in the forest when it's too dark to continue. The Voildi are on edge out here, with most of them talking in low voices. Zoey is dumped next to me, and I make her drink some water, then attempt to get her to eat some of the meat the Voildi hand us.

Thankfully, I saw five or six Voildi leave the camp before returning with a huge animal that they slaughtered and cooked.

Best to know where your food is coming from when you're eating with cannibals.

I snort. Maybe when I'm back on Earth, I can put that on a T-shirt.

Zoey falls asleep almost instantly, curled up next to me. We're lying slightly closer to the fire tonight, and I listen to the Voildi talking amongst themselves as my eyes grow heavy. The word *Braxians* is mentioned multiple times, and from what I've gathered, they're the warriors who attacked the Voildi when we were first taken and before these guys kidnapped us.

The Braxians were huge, muscled, and lethal. I saw them fight briefly before we were taken, and there's nothing I'd like more than for a few of them to stumble across us and take the Voildi down.

Although, let's face it—the last time we were "rescued" on this planet, it didn't really go all that well for us. It's likely that we're better off staying away from any and all aliens on Agron.

Killis seems to have chosen his spot well, and there are no Braxians finding us anytime soon. He seems pleased the next morning, and I'm kicked awake as soon as there's enough light to start walking again.

"Should we leave this one?" A Voildi gestures to Zoey, who just stares at him, her eyes clouded with pain.

"No," Killis snaps.

"She's weak and will slow us down."

"Someone will buy her." Killis turns his back dismissively, and the Voildi growls, gesturing for Zoey to get to her feet.

"Ouch," I murmur. "Your friend gets left behind to die, but you have to take a stranger with you? That's gotta sting."

He narrows his eyes, reaching out to hit me, and I raise my hands, which are thankfully no longer tied. Another Voildi moves closer, muttering something to him, and his face goes blank as he lifts Zoey, once again throwing her over his shoulder.

We reach some kind of village at dusk. Most of the houses have been constructed with whatever material the owners can find, and they look like they'd fall over at the first storm. A few of them appear to have been painstakingly built out of wood, with a window in each wall, and they're obviously the homes of the wealthier residents around here.

People come to their doors as we walk past. Most of them stare at Zoey and me curiously, but none dare to approach the Voildi, many of them dropping their eyes or returning inside. I can see why. These people have nothing, and while Killis left the Voildi women and children with some guards back at the cave, this is still a massive group. Something tells me that the Voildi have a reputation for being assholes on this planet.

From what I can gather, Killis was hoping to sell us at a slave market around here, but the Braxians shut it down. This news led to a lot of pacing and screaming from Killis, which provided me with plenty of entertainment. These Braxians are quickly becoming some of my favorite people.

Killis turns to one of the Voildi close to me. "Has it been done?"

"Yes, milord. Havish sent word that they have taken over the houses you specified."

"Good."

CHAPTER TWO

V^{rex}

I scowl into the forest. It's getting dark, and the sooner I can finish this task, the sooner I can return to my tashiv.

"Come out, Maxis. I know you're here."

"Vrex?" His voice holds a sliver of fear, and I sigh.

"Yes."

"Thane sent you after me? After all I've done for him, he sent the Assassin of Agron?"

I grind my teeth at the nickname. "I'm not going to kill you," I say. "Unless you force me to," I clarify, and his snort reaches my ears.

"I'm not going back."

"Thane doesn't want you dead," I say, my tone bored. A branch cracks, and I sigh. Maxis is attempting to escape. He seems to have forgotten that I spent most of my life in the wild. He may also be a Braxian warrior, but according to his tribe king, he prefers to spend his time in his camp.

I slowly circle, my feet soft as I use the light of the moon to avoid stepping on anything that might give away my position. Maxis chooses silence, but I'm standing downwind, and I get a whiff of unwashed male.

You should have paid more attention to hygiene, Maxis.

My senses are heightened after a lifetime of hunting in the forests of Agron, and I creep closer, finding Maxis with his back to a tree, his sword in his hand as he bares his teeth in the darkness.

I don't feel the need to drag this out. Maxis tenses further at a sound to his right, and I use the opportunity to silently circle around behind him.

When I am almost close enough to touch him, my boot hits a rock, all of my attention on the warrior in front of me. He begins to turn, and I lunge forward, slamming the hilt of my sword into his temple.

He hits the ground, and I lift my fingers to my mouth, letting a whistle loose.

Nari appears, her feet almost silent as she moves through the forest. A lifetime of hunting with me has taught the mishua the importance of staying quiet.

She snorts at Maxis as I take his sword before deftly tying his hands and feet.

I gesture, and she hesitates.

"I know," I say, "but there's no other way to get him back to his camp. You'd like to go home, wouldn't you?"

The mishua lets out a sigh and lowers herself until I can drag the other warrior onto her back. I leave him hanging over the saddle in front of me so I can stop him if he regains consciousness and attempts to flee.

Thane meets me at his camp gates when I arrive. I encourage Nari to kneel again, and she complies, drawing gasps from Thane's warriors.

Most Braxians have never seen a mishua cooperate in this way, but Nari and I have a bond that is closer than most.

I push Maxis off the mishua, and he rolls to the ground with a groan. Thane stares down at him coldly and then meets my gaze as Nari gets to her feet.

"Thank you for your service," he says stiffly, and I nod.

"Planning to tell me what he did?"

"After drinking too much noptri, he attempted to take an unwilling female to his furs. That female is my daughter."

I almost wince but manage to keep my face blank. Honor is everything amongst my people, regardless of their tribe. If Thane allows Maxis to live, the warrior will likely wish he had not.

"Your payment," Thane says, throwing a cloth bag to me. I catch it, feeling the weight of the credits. Impressive. It's the words he will speak next that I truly value, however.

Thane raises his voice. "I swear to give you one favor, taken at a time of your choosing. Provided that no harm will come to me and mine with this favor, of course."

I nod and turn my head. Nari moves, and we leave Maxis to his fate, with yet another assignment completed.

And another favor added.

Ivy

I shift on the cold floor, staring through the bars of my cage. I keep track of the days by scratching tallies in the wall behind it.

We've been here for two weeks.

Zoey's cage is next to mine, and she spends most of her time curled into a ball.

I try to bully her into eating, but from the sweat on her forehead, she has a fever. Combine that with the rib injuries, and it's likely pneumonia.

Frustration and rage war within me. I need to get her out of here and to whatever passes for a doctor on this planet. Unfortunately, this cage may be made from wood, but no matter how much I kick at the thick slats, they refuse to break.

We've been crated. Like dogs.

The Voildi ignore us for the most part. Twice a day, we're taken to the bathroom, and every second day, one of the Voildi ensures that there is a bucket of cold water in the bathroom so we can wash.

Ironic, considering how badly the Voildi smell, but it makes sense considering Killis is currently in negotiations to sell us.

The Voildi is reading a piece of paper right now, his gaze so intent that I half expect him to start sounding out the words.

"They want to come *here?*" he asks the Voildi who I've mentally dubbed Hook. The Voildi is missing most of his fingers, and his remaining finger and thumb are clutched around a sharp hook, which he uses to carry out everyday tasks.

"Yes, milord. The Zintas have crossed the Colossal Water to trade on this part of Agron. One of their leaders has learned of the human females and is curious. He expressed his interest but only if he can see them first."

I silently grind my teeth. One thing's for sure: I have zero interest in crossing the Colossal Water. And I doubt Zoey would even survive such a trip.

Killis is silent for a moment, then turns his head, scanning us both. "He may come. Only him. The Zintas are dangerous, and if we are not careful, they may decide to simply kill us and take the females."

I snarl at him, and he smiles back at me before returning his attention to Hook.

"I want them sold. Quickly. Before the weak one dies. I'm tired of waiting, and we need payment so we can afford more weapons."

Hook nods. "I will make your wishes known, milord."

I slump in my cage. If we're sold, at least we'll have an opportunity to escape.

Killis and Hook leave, and I move closer to Zoey, keeping my voice low even though the room is empty.

"Did you hear that, Zo? We may be getting out of here."

"Yeah, before the weak one dies." Zoey's voice is a hoarse whisper, and I reach my hand between the bars, angling my arm until I can brush the hair off her face.

"Let them underestimate you," I tell her. "'He will win who, prepared himself, waits to take the enemy unprepared.'"

Zoey shifts, getting slowly to her knees. "Is that from the bible or something?"

"*The Art of War*. And we're going to take these bastards down."

She smiles, but it doesn't reach her eyes. "I need you to promise me something," she wheezes.

"Zoey—"

"Shh. You know what I'm going to say. The exact same thing you said to Beth. You see an opportunity, you take it."

"No."

"What happened to 'We do whatever is best for all of us. If even one of us can escape, we can get help for the others,' huh?"

I scowl. "That's some memory you've got there. It's different now."

"Because I'm dying."

"You're not dying."

"Did you forget our conversation when I told you I'm a nurse?"

I sigh. No, I didn't. We don't chat much, but we've shared enough that I know that Zoey is from New York too, and I often bring patients to the hospital she works at. It's a small universe.

"Fine," I say. "*If* I have a chance to escape, I'll take it, and I promise I'll bring back help."

Zoey nods, slowly lying back down. That simple conversation seems to have exhausted her, and I pass the next few minutes by kicking at the wooden slats of my cage again.

A shadow appears in the doorway, and I freeze, my hands behind my butt, feet still poised in the air. The shadow moves, and I gulp at the huge creature, who strides into the room, unexpectedly quick given his size.

"Aroth," Killis says, his tone surprisingly diffident, "we believe you will enjoy these alien females."

Aroth's claws remind me of Wolverine's, and his body is covered in...fur. From the way the creature is scanning my body, I'm guessing that he's the Zinta that Killis was talking about.

I shift until I'm leaning against the back wall of my cage, but the furry monster drops to his knees, peering in at me.

"Flame Hair," he rumbles. "Take her out."

Killis is standing behind the Zinta, and he nods toward Hook, who moves forward, unlatching my cage and opening the door.

"Out," Killis orders, and I stay where I am.

Aroth laughs, seemingly delighted with my defiance. He leans down, reaches into the cage, and drags me out.

I fight, but the guy probably has a solid two hundred pounds on me, if not more. As soon as I'm standing, he steps back, running his gaze over me.

His eyes are a deep green, cold and shrewd. His head is also covered in fur, although it's thinner around the center of his face.

"Like what you see, Flame Hair?"

I raise one eyebrow. "I've never seen a talking bear before. Forgive me for staring."

Unless they have bears on this planet, he won't get the reference, and yet he seems to understand that he's been insulted. He grins at me, displaying sharp white teeth.

"I like her," he tells Killis, and I mentally kick myself.

"What about the other one?"

I glance at where Zoey is curled up in her cage, making herself as small as possible.

"I can smell sickness on her," Aroth says.

Killis lets out a low growl, and the Zinta turns to him, raising his eyebrow.

"I have business here in Nexia, and also in Malufic later today. You will take the female to Malufic, and I will take her from there."

"I'm not leaving Zoey," I say, and everyone ignores me. Aroth reaches out to touch my hair, and I bat away his hand with a curse. He laughs, and I realize he's getting off on the fact that I want nothing to do with him. This doesn't bode well for me.

Hook shoves me back in my cage as the males discuss payment. For me. I'm going to need some solid time in the dentist's chair when I get back to Earth. My teeth will probably be nothing but stubs after all this grinding.

They all leave the room, and I pound at the wooden slats in my cage.

"What the hell did they reinforce this thing with?" I snarl. "Concrete?"

Zoey is quiet beside me, and I glance over to see her facing me, her eyes serious.

"You know what to do," she says. "This is your chance."

I slam my fist into the cage, but it doesn't make me feel any better.

"Come back for me," she whispers. "I want to die with the sun on my face."

"You're not dying," I growl. "But I'll get help and come back. I promise."

We're quiet for the next few hours until another Voildi returns. I haven't seen this one around, and he seems bored as he unlocks my cage and gestures for me to get out.

I get to my feet, my head down, shoulders hunched. The Voildi reaches for my arm, and I swing my other fist at his jaw. It connects, and he shouts as his head slams back into the wall. I shove past him, but Voildi are pouring into the room. I meet Zoey's gaze, and she gives me a tiny grin before I'm dragged away.

Ivy

Killis comes with us to Malufic. Hook keeps a close eye on me, and I grin at him, wincing as the movement stretches my split lip.

My escape attempt wasn't productive, but it sure was fun.

We've been walking for a few hours now. Killis left most

of the Voildi back with Zoey, and I stayed quiet enough that they must've almost forgotten I was here as they cursed the Braxians. From what I can tell, the Voildi can't afford to travel in a massive pack in this area because if the Braxians find them, they'll take them all out.

Wouldn't that be nice.

Unfortunately, it doesn't look like there will be any huge alien warriors coming to my rescue.

That's okay. My dad taught me to rescue myself.

I swallow around a lump in my throat. When you lose someone you love, you never truly get over it. You'll think you're doing just fine until you're blindsided by the inescapable fact that you'll never laugh with that person again. Never fight with them. Never tell them you love them. Never describe your alien abduction.

I snort. Dad would have a lot to say about this, that's for sure. My father was a quiet man until someone gave him something to rant about. He taught me to fight, showed me how to live, and believed in preparation above almost anything else.

If my dad were here now, he'd tell me to wait for my chance. There's always an opportunity somewhere—I just need to be ready to take it.

Eventually, the Voildi begin to relax, and we move out of the depths of the forest and into another village. This one is in slightly better condition than the last, and we stop at a two-story gray building that backs onto the forest.

Killis nods at Hook, who opens the door and gestures for me to go upstairs. I move slowly up the stairs, looking for any opportunity to escape, but there's nothing. The stairs lead to a small hallway with two doors.

"Open the door on the right," Hook says, and I comply. The room is large, with a single window open to the forest outside, although I notice nothing but the cage in the corner.

I don't fucking think so.

Hook leans down to unlatch the cage door. I don't hesitate, slamming my fist down on the back of his neck. He curses, landing on his knees, and I jump on his back, wrapping my arm around his neck.

Here's hoping that the Voildi have at least a few things in common with humans. No matter the species, surely everyone's brains need oxygen...right?

I pull up on Hook's neck, squeezing tight, and he lashes out, dragging his hook down my thigh.

Son of a bitch.

His good hand comes up to claw at the arm I've wrapped around his neck, while his hook swings for me again. I manage to block it with my knee, heart pounding as he slumps closer to the ground, the hook falling from his hand.

My mouth goes dry as fear makes me dizzy. If they heard that downstairs, they'll be coming up here within seconds.

"Hurry up, damn you," I hiss.

Hook's face is bright yellow now, and we both hit the ground as he face-plants. I keep my arm tightly wrapped around his neck for a few more seconds just in case he's faking, and then I pick up the hook, getting to my feet.

If I had time, I'd lock this bastard in that cage. See how he likes it.

Instead, I close the door enough that it hides Hook's body and position myself behind it, clutching the sharp metal hook tightly in my hand.

Not even thirty seconds later, someone pushes open the door, and I jump out from my hiding spot.

Killis whirls, but I'm already there, slashing at him with the sharp hook. He raises his hands, but it's too late, and his scream is chilling as the pointed metal rips into his forehead before dragging down his face.

"My eye!" Killis roars, cupping his face.

I don't hang around. I'm already moving, heading for the window. I scan the ground below me for a single second before I jump, praying I won't break an ankle or dislocate a knee when I land.

It hurts, my left ankle immediately letting me know that it's not happy. My thigh howls at me, but I launch straight into a limping run, my chest tight as Killis screams at his men to follow me.

I tuck my chin down, find my stride, and keep running.

CHAPTER THREE

V rex

War is coming.

Fortunes will be won and lost. People will die, and history will be forever changed on this planet after the events of the next few days.

I can't say exactly why I came to Tecar's tribe. Perhaps, in the back of my mind, I sensed an opportunity to negotiate for yet another favor.

Or perhaps I simply became tired of conversing with no one but my mishua and occasionally the various people I pay to spy for me.

There's a sense of excitement in the air as I make my way through the tribe, my mishua demanding a large space around her as she moves. Nari snorts at a warrior who is slow to move out of the way, and the warrior grins at me. I nod back, finally spotting Rakiz in the distance.

Rakiz lifts his brow as I dismount.

"Who sent a messenger to you?" he asks, neither of us fond of pleasantries.

"I chose to come."

He nods, and a strange female moves closer. This must be one of the humans I have heard so much about. My assignments require me to keep up to date with what is happening on this planet, and I have heard plenty about the huge ship that crashed near the Seinex Forest and the strange, small females who were taken by the Voildi.

"Sup," the female says. The implant in my ear translates this to mean eating, and I frown, confused, but say nothing. My silence does not appear to disconcert the female, who is dressed in warrior's pants.

"Thanks for coming," she says, glancing at Rakiz. He reaches out to pull her to him, and I raise my eyebrow. Even Rakiz has mated. And with an alien female no less.

"Can I interrupt for a moment?" the female asks.

Rakiz gazes into his mate's eyes. "Of course," he says, and the female smiles at him.

"I'd like to hire you," the female says to me, and Rakiz looks surprised by this but stays silent.

I stroke my mishua. I think I can guess what it is this female wants from me, but I ask anyway, "What task is it that you need?"

"Karja," Rakiz says, and I tilt my head. Karja are dangerous animals on this planet, and yet the tribe king has named his mate after them.

The female raises her hand to Rakiz's face, and the crowd is silent as they seem to have a wordless conversation.

"I need to do this," the female says. "Please."

Rakiz nods, and I narrow my eyes, mentally filing away this interaction to analyze later.

Rakiz's mate glances at another female, who steps

forward. The warrior closest to her sends me a warning look, and I almost snort. These warriors may choose to fear for their own lives when I'm around, but they have no need to fear that I will steal their females. I learned young that a mate and children are not for me.

"We are from another planet," the second female says. "We were separated from each other, and I was kidnapped by the Voildi along with two other women. One of them is safe now, but the other one is responsible for the damage to Killis's eye."

I tilt my head at this. Everyone on this part of the planet has heard of what happened to Killis's eye. And it is a rare person who would feel any sympathy for the Voildi. It would take a fierce female to accomplish injuring Killis.

Rakiz's mate clears her throat. "Her name is Ivy. She was last seen running through the prexas after she escaped from the Voildi. Will you help us find her?"

The females are so tense that they seem to barely breathe as they wait for my answer.

I take a moment to consider it. Truthfully, I have no need to earn another favor from Rakiz. However, some instinct inside me is urging me to agree to this task.

I have learned to always listen to my instincts.

Rakiz meets my gaze, and I raise my eyebrow.

"If I do this, you will owe me one favor, due at the time of my choosing."

The king's jaw tightens, but he nods, and I bow my head. "It is done."

The females walk away, and Rakiz watches his queen as she laughs with one of the warriors.

A mate is not for a male like me, but that doesn't mean I don't wonder what it would be like to have a female of my own.

Rakiz turns to me. "We saved Zoey—one of the females who was taken. The Voildi had almost killed her, and she is still recovering at my camp. But the other female is nowhere to be found. Do you believe you can find her?"

"I would not agree to this task if I did not believe I could do it. There are only so many places an alien female could be in that area, particularly if she has no credits."

Rakiz tilts his head. "These females are not like any females you have encountered before," he warns me.

I snort. "You may be enchanted with your new mate, Rakiz, but that does not mean that this female will present any kind of challenge."

The tribe king stares at me for a long moment, and then a slow smile spreads over his face.

"Good luck, Vrex," he says softly.

***

Ivy

I sprint through the forest, well aware that the Voildi will be hunting me. And after that little incident with Killis, he may decide that the pleasure he'll get from killing and eating me is worth more to him than any money he'll get for selling me.

Ugh.

I jump over a fallen tree and wince. I rolled my left ankle when I leaped out of that second-story window. I'll need to suck it up though 'cause I can already hear the Voildi shouting as they chase me.

The air is cool on my face as I run. I probably only have a few hours of daylight left, and I need to find somewhere I can hunker down overnight.

I have no idea where I am. The forest looks the same from every angle, the trees close enough that I almost brain myself on a branch as I whirl, looking for some kind of path.

"The wise warrior avoids the battle."

Tzu was right about that. And if there's one thing I can do, it's run. Even in my half-starved state, with a messed-up ankle, a bleeding thigh, and no shoes, I feel confident that I can run for miles. The problem? I don't know if the Voildi can also do the same. And since they hunt in a pack, they may find a way to trap me.

I scan my surroundings. Distantly, I can hear the rush of water, which could be some kind of river. Getting wet right before the temperature drops and the sun disappears is not a good idea, however. The trees are high, but even if I climb one of them, I'll be trapped up there if the Voildi find me.

My heart pounds as I hear them get closer. I'm sucking air so quickly that I'm close to hyperventilation, and I make an effort to match my breath to my strides.

I need somewhere to hide.

I move further toward where I can hear water. At the very least, the sound of the river may cover up the noise I'm making as I crash through the forest.

"Shit!"

I barely manage to make it to a stop before I fall into a hole in the ground. It appeared out of nowhere—perfectly round and without any markers explaining what the hell it could be.

The Voildi are getting closer, and my mouth goes dry. If it's some huge animal's lair, I'm about to become dinner, but at this point, I'll take any hiding spot I can get.

I peer down the hole, and the breath leaves my lungs in a rush. I'm staring at a ladder, and there's a dim light glowing from within the cave.

At this point, I have no choice. I twist in place before descending the ladder quickly and drop to my feet as soon as I can see the ground in front of me.

I'm about eight feet below the entrance to the cave, which is not a cave at all but a tunnel.

I don't hesitate. I sprint away from the ladder, desperate to put some distance between myself and the Voildi.

There are only a few things in life that I'm certain of, but I know for damn sure that I'm not going to be sold to a huge, furry asshole on an alien planet.

I'm still clutching the hook in my hand, and it glints at me in the low light, covered in Killis's blood. And likely some of mine. A weapon is a weapon at this point, but I'd give anything for a gun.

I snort. The Arcav outlawed guns on Earth years ago. It was one of the first things they did when they invaded.

I haven't held a gun in my hand since I went hunting with my dad when I was a kid.

Still, any kind of weapon would be welcome right now.

I can hear voices, and I slow as I come to an intersection. To the right, It sounds like a group of males are having some kind of argument, and things are getting heated. There's a loud thump, followed by a high-pitched scream, and I shiver.

That's a nope from me.

I head to the left, picking up the pace. Obviously, these underground tunnels are well known on this planet. That means that when the Voildi can't find me aboveground, they'll be coming after me down here.

And I bet they know where these tunnels lead.

The tunnel suddenly opens up to some kind of room, with multiple other tunnels leading off it. I survey the people in the room—a woman with dark-blue skin and a Voildi, who narrows his eyes at me.

I raise my rust-stained hook threateningly.

"There is no violence in the trading posts," the woman says, moving slightly closer. "Those who break this rule are punished by the creatures who call this region their home."

The Voildi sneers at me but turns to leave. I make a mental note not to choose that tunnel in case he's waiting for me. He's dressed differently to the other Voildi, wearing nothing but a thin loincloth, but who's to say they're not working together?

"So violence in the tunnels is A-okay, but these rooms are off-limits?"

She nods. "The prexas, yes. The trading posts are neutral ground."

"Do you know which one of these prexas will get me away from this area and aboveground?"

She runs her eyes over me, pausing at my hair. While this planet may be kicking *my* ass, she looks beaten down by life. Her dark eyes have circles under them, and her shoulders are hunched as if she needs to constantly protect herself from the world.

"That one," she murmurs, pointing to a prexa on the opposite side of the trading post, next to the one the Voildi chose. "Follow it until you get to the fifth intersection and then go right. Three intersections later, turn to the left and keep going until you find the exit."

"Thank you," I murmur. "I appreciate it."

"Good luck," she says, her eyes already moving past me as someone else enters the trading post.

I don't stick around.

"Right at the fifth intersection, left three intersections later," I repeat to myself as I break into a jog.

Over the next couple of hours, I alternate between running and walking—needing to conserve my strength but feeling increasingly desperate to get out of here. These tunnels—prexas—go on for miles, and I'd give just about anything for a breath of fresh air at this point.

There are more voices up ahead, but I'm not turning back now. I don't slow down, and I'm running through the third intersection when the breath is forced from my lungs as I'm suddenly slammed against the wall.

The creature has dark-gray skin, and his breath smells like a sewer. He bares his teeth in a grin as he leans down, trapping me against the dirt wall.

"You look different," he grins. "Where did you come from, strange female?"

I wrestle with disbelief. A guy who looks like a leathery gray tortoise is calling *me* strange?

"Oh, you know, here and there. Take your hands off me before you lose them."

He throws his head back and laughs. "You are funny, strange female. We will get many credits for you at the market."

I glance over his shoulder, my heart sinking. There are two more tortoise men behind him, all wearing the same shit-eating grin.

"Market's shut down," I say. "You may need to rethink that plan."

The man studies me out of black eyes, and I clutch my hook. I'll never forget what it was like to be stolen by the Grivath and sold like a piece of meat. That will *never* happen to me again.

I clench my hand even tighter around my hook, the metal warm in my sweaty hand.

"Let her go," a deep voice says, and the tortoise men all

turn their heads. I crane my neck until I can see the outline of a huge male, his face shadowed by the light glowing behind him.

"We found her first. This is no concern of yours, Braxian."

My heart pounds faster. Braxian? They're the race that the Voildi are so scared of. If he can distract these assholes, I can get the hell out of here. Here's hoping that the enemy of my enemy really is my friend.

CHAPTER FOUR

V^{rex}

There's no question that this is the female I have been looking for.

Her hair spills over her shoulders, the ends in tangles, but it still glows like fire in the low light. Her eyes are wary as she stares at me, and her lip is bleeding. I suddenly feel an urgent need to force the Kusa to take his hands off her.

"We found her first," he says again, returning his attention to the female. She scowls at him, and I step closer as the light catches on something sharp in her hand.

"Vrex," one of the other Kusa says as he recognizes my face, and this time, there's a shard of fear in his voice.

I nod. "You know who I am. Think carefully about what you will do next."

The male steps back, eyes darting. The Kusa pinning the human female to the wall snorts, lifting a piece of her hair between his claws and examining it idly.

"This isn't your territory, Braxian. I suggest you go back aboveground, where you belong."

The female stares at me coolly, raising her eyebrow. From the expression on her face and the weapon clutched in her hand, she's waiting for me to make a move.

I narrow my eyes back at her.

Don't try anything, female.

"Herz, you know who he is? This here is the Assassin of Agron. You want to mess with him, go ahead. I'm out of here." The Kusa wisely takes off, abandoning his friends. The other Kusa snorts as his friend leaves, choosing instead to elbow past Herz and stare me down.

My gaze drops to the mace in his hand. A difficult weapon to use in such close quarters. He has a knife in his other hand, however.

"We found her first," he spits out, striding forward with a swagger.

I say nothing, staring at him silently. Most people cannot deal with silence. They must immediately fill it with their ramblings.

This Kusa is no different.

"I'm going to make you bleed," he sneers. I keep my face blank, and my lack of response pushes him over the edge. He steps closer, and the light glints off the blade in his right hand. He's faster than I expected, the knife stabbing the air close to my chest as I move, wishing these prexas were wider.

I hate being underground.

I grab his wrist, taking the knife from him, and he drops into a crouch, swinging the mace wildly. Ivy gasps, and I glance at her, but the other Kusa is still and silent as he watches his friend.

I kick out. The Kusa rolls back, jumping to his feet, teeth

bared. I spin, blocking the trajectory of the mace, but the Kusa charges toward me, using the mace's momentum to pull it back for another swing. It hits my collarbone, and my vision turns black for a long moment as pain shudders through my body.

The Kusa is off-balance, and I thrust his knife into his neck.

He falls to his feet, and I meet Herz's eyes. His brow creases as he glares at me, ignoring his friend as he chokes on his own blood.

"I suggest you let me go," the female says suddenly, drawing his attention back to her. I step closer.

Herz is no longer amused, his expression hard. "And why would I do that?"

The female lashes out with the weapon in her hand. Herz raises an arm, not expecting the flash of silver, and the female uses the opportunity to punch him in the throat with her other hand, smoothly sliding under his arm as I stalk forward, placing my sword against his throat.

"Leave," I say as Herz coughs, massaging his throat. He glares at us but doesn't argue, slinking down the prexa toward the smarter one of his friends.

"So," the female says, her gaze dropping to the Kusa slumped on the ground. "The Assassin of Agron, huh?"

Strangely, the title coming from her lips feels worse than it felt coming from Maxis, who was convinced I was there to kill him.

"Vrex," I say, and she nods.

"I'm Ivy. Thanks for the help. Much appreciated. I'll just be on my way."

My mouth almost drops open as she nods at me, turning to stride down the prexa in the opposite direction of the Kusas.

Insane female.

I follow her, and after just a few steps, she glowers over her shoulder at me.

"Let me be real clear, Mr. Stalker. I'm not in the mood."

"I can help you," I growl, shaking my head incredulously when the female—Ivy, I remember—simply snorts and continues walking.

I scratch my head as I watch her, and then, with no idea what to do next, I follow her down the prexa.

She seems to know where she's going, continuing until she eventually turns left. At this rate, we'll exit the prexas close to my mishua. I'll just need to somehow convince her to get on that mishua with me.

Other than a few wary glances thrown over her shoulder, Ivy ignores me. This is new. Creatures on this planet have many different reactions when I am near. Fear, loathing, anxiety—they are all to be expected. This female's reaction is not usual. At all.

Rakiz's words float through my mind.

These females are not like any females you have encountered before.

Perhaps. But the way that this female is taking the utmost care to pretend I don't exist is still entirely unexpected.

We walk through the prexa, encountering many of the creatures here. All of them stare at the strange alien female before shifting their eyes to mine and quickly glancing away. Ivy seems to note this, a hint of gratitude in her eyes as she glances back at me.

Maybe she believes my presence is good for something.

Eventually, we come to the prexa's exit, and every muscle in my body tightens when the female climbs up the ladder, her curvy ass highlighted by the strange, thin, torn clothes she wears.

When I reach the top of the ladder, she's glancing around, obviously with no idea where to go next.

"Female," I say, and she raises her eyebrow again. Her skin is creamy and smooth, and there are tiny freckles scattered across her face. My eyes cling to one that's a little darker than the others, positioned next to her mouth.

"My name is Ivy," she says.

"Ivy. I am here to help."

"An assassin wants to help me?" Her tone is lightly sarcastic, but her gaze is still cautious as she scans my body.

"I am not *just* an assassin," I say tightly.

She smiles, and the breath leaves my lungs as the freckle is replaced by the dimple that appears next to her mouth.

"What are you, then?"

"I am someone who does things that others either can't or don't want to do," I say.

The humor leaves her face, and I feel my brows draw together as it's replaced by pity.

"Okay, then," she says gently. "So for some reason, you'd like to collect some karma and help me?"

I do not know what karma is, but I do want to help her. "Yes."

"You feel like being my hero?"

Her tone is light, but the hope in her eyes... I find myself unwilling to tell her that I was sent by another to help her. For once, I would like to be someone's *hero*. Even if it is just temporary.

I nod.

"Okay, then. In that case, we can start by going back to where my friend Zoey is being kept."

"Why don't you tell me how you escaped first?"

Ivy complies, turning to pace as she describes being separated from her friend and attacking the Voildi before jumping out of a window. I drop my gaze to her small white feet, which are covered in scratches and bruises amongst the dirt.

"So you see, I need to go back and find Zoey."

"Do you know where she was kept?"

Her face turns blank, frustration in her eyes. "It was a small village. The houses were tiny and looked like they'd blow over with the first wind."

"This could be many places in this area. I can help you find her, but we will need more warriors to join us."

I gesture to my collarbone, and her eyes darken with sympathy.

"After your escape, the Voildi will have increased the number of guards on your friend. It will be difficult for me to kill all of them and carry your friend with only one fighting arm."

"I can help."

I keep my face blank. Females do not fight.

She narrows her eyes at me, seemingly reading my mind. "What do you suggest?" she bites out. "I can't just leave her there."

"You can tell me everything you remember about the area where you and your friend were kept before you were separated. We will travel back to my tashiv, and I will send a message to an acquaintance, asking him to send some warriors to help us."

She thinks on this for a moment, a tiny line appearing between her brows. "I know it makes sense," she mutters finally. "But I don't want to leave her."

"You have already left her," I say, and she flinches. I

silently curse. I have never had the correct words to say to females, and this female is no different.

"It's not just Zoey," she says. "Our friend Beth managed to escape and never returned with help. I know she would've come back if she could have. I need to find her as well."

"The territory surrounding this area is home to a tribe that is not an ally to the tribes I am allied to. If we are found here, we will be in severe danger. You cannot help your friends if you are dead."

She stares at me for a long moment, her gaze lingering on my collarbone. I grit my teeth against the pain as I wait for her to make a decision. Truthfully, there is only one choice for her to make, and if I need to tie her to my mishua to force her cooperation, that is what I will do.

I have done worse.

The female seems to see the resolve on my face because her eyes become slits as she stares at me.

"Fine," she finally says. "Let's go get some more help."

Ivy

I work with a lot of big guys. You have to be strong to be a firefighter.

But this alien makes them look like prepubescent boys.

Vrex lifts his good hand, letting out a loud whistle. Then his dark eyes examine me as he waits for God only knows what.

He's a good-looking man. Even with the long, winding scar that trails across his forehead.

He's probably got at least a foot on me, and from the look of his bulging muscles, he could likely bench-press my body without any effort. His hair is dark, hanging slightly past his shoulders and braided back from his face. He has a smudge of dirt on his chin, and I have the weirdest urge to wipe it away.

His eyes are a dark brown, shuttered and inscrutable.

He's hiding something from me. For sure. After everything I've been through since I was taken from Earth, I'm in no hurry to trust an enigmatic stranger who *says* he's here to help me.

But at the same time, there's no doubt that he really did save my bacon back in those prexas. And I don't really have all that many options available to me.

Choices, choices.

Vrex shifts on his feet, glancing over his shoulder, and I don't miss the slight wince on his face. I broke my collarbone a few years ago when a wooden beam collapsed in a warehouse as we searched for anyone who could be trapped.

It was pure agony. There's no way to wrap a cast around a collarbone, so the pain was excruciating as the broken bone shifted with even the tiniest movement.

This guy is handling it like a champ. If I didn't know better, I'd think I was in more pain with my twisted ankle.

Something moves between the trees, and I tense, but Vrex doesn't look at all concerned. He shifts impatiently, and my mouth drops open as a four-legged lizard creature appears.

It's covered in dark-green scales, although if I just looked at its furry legs, I'd think it was an oversize wolf. Its head is covered in huge white horns, and it stares at me through dark-red eyes.

"What the fuck is that?"

Vrex tilts his head. "This is my mishua."

"Mishua?"

He nods and gently strokes the beast as it moves closer, nuzzling at him.

"I'll walk."

His eyes lighten with amusement. "We don't have time. We must be gone from this territory before dark."

"I'll take my chances."

He raises one eyebrow, smoothly sidestepping to protect his bad arm as the mishua disregards his personal space. "You escaped a pack of Voildi and braved the prexas alone, but the mishua frightens you?"

I scowl at him. "I had no choice about the other things. I have no desire to end up an Ivy kebab when that thing skewers me with its horns."

"Her name is Nari."

Of course. Because why wouldn't a giant killing machine be called something sweet and unassuming like Nari?

Vrex gestures to the mishua, and she lowers herself to the ground.

"I won't let her hurt you," he promises me in his low voice. Strangely, I trust him. In this, at least.

"Fine," I sigh. "But if I get impaled before I can escape this planet, I'm gonna be real pissy."

Vrex holds out his hand, and I move closer, careful to keep the huge guy between me and the mishua's head. The lizard-wolf seems to find this amusing, because she lets out a snort and tosses her head, still staring at me.

"No sudden movements," I murmur to myself. But I take Vrex's good hand as he helps me onto the leather saddle. He slides in behind me, and I curse, scrabbling for something to hold on to as the animal gets to her feet.

Vrex shows me where to put my hands—apparently the beast will be just fine with me clutching at one of the horns sticking out from her neck.

"This doesn't seem safe," I mutter.

Vrex simply lets out a low chuckle, and the mishua begins to walk.

Within a few minutes, I've settled into her long-legged stride.

How did I end up here? On an alien planet, on the run from fuckwits who want to sell me?

The last thing I remember on Earth is drinking copious amounts of wine after Steve broke up with me. Over the phone.

"This isn't working," he'd said. "I love you, but I can't do this any longer. You're never home, and when you're at work, I never know if someone's going to knock on the door and tell me that you've gone down in the line."

I grind my teeth. Two years we were together. And he couldn't even tell me it was over to my face. The ironic part? I knew I was better off alone. Steve spent six months convincing me to go on a date with him before I gave in. And it was just two years before the reality of my life slapped him in the face.

I have no idea how the Grivath took me. I wasn't rostered on that night, so I was at home, in the Brooklyn apartment that had suddenly become half empty while I was at the firehouse.

When I woke up on that spaceship, I actually laughed. You think a breakup is bad? Try getting abducted by aliens and sold on a slave planet.

"How many other females are there like you on this planet?" Vrex asks, dragging me from my thoughts.

"Um, I think there were around eight or nine of us. We

all got separated when a few guys like you appeared and attacked the Voildi."

He nods, and we travel in silence for a few more minutes.

"Where do you live anyway?" I ask.

"My tashiv is close to the Seinex Forest."

"Tashiv?"

"It is my home. I prefer my privacy."

I nod. Great. Follow the huge warrior to his remote forest lair, Ivy. That's never ended badly.

Strangely, I don't think Vrex will hurt me. He's definitely a man of few words, and I wouldn't give him points for charm. But if he wanted to take me out, he could've done it at any time before now.

Unless he's waiting to rape and murder you in solitude.

I almost snort. This guy is definitely hiding something from me, but I don't think he's the type to go to all this trouble just to hurt me.

I'm not an idiot though. I'll still keep an eye on him just in case.

CHAPTER FIVE

I vy

When this guy said he had a home in the woods, I was expecting a shack like the tiny houses in the town where Zoey and I were kept.

"Wow," I murmur as Vrex makes the mishua kneel again and helps me off her back. "This is gorgeous."

His face is still blank as he gazes at the huge log cabin sprawling in front of us, but somehow, I can sense his pride at my words.

"Thank you."

I can hear the crashing of water nearby. Other than the sound of the water splashing over rocks and the call of birds in the trees surrounding the clearing, there's nothing but sweet, sweet silence.

I'm about as far from Brooklyn as I can get.

I shift my attention back to Vrex. "How long did this take you to build?"

"Two revolutions."

I'm guessing he means two years. And it's easy to see how it would take at least that long. From what I've seen of this planet so far, I'm doubting that there were any cranes or other machinery to help. No, Vrex built this entirely with his hands.

"Did you build this alone?"

A single sharp nod. He leads the mishua to a small pen and takes off her saddle, rubbing her down with a murmur. I watch as the fearsome beast becomes about as cuddly as a kitten. She's practically purring as he grabs a cloth sack, maneuvering it with his good hand so he can pour some kind of food into a long wooden trough.

When he's done, his dark gaze scans the area around us.

"You shouldn't walk around here by yourself," he says, and I raise an eyebrow.

"Why?"

"I have built many different traps to protect my territory from predators. If you take the wrong path, you may end up hurt or worse."

I shiver at that, once again questioning the wisdom of following a strange man back to his cabin in the woods. He seems to read my mind, his eyes lightening in amusement.

"I won't hurt you," he says.

"I'm sure Bundy said the same thing," I mutter, but I can't help but smile at his confused frown. "Listen," I continue. "When can we get a message to your friend? We need to ask him to send us some backup so we can rescue Zoey."

"The trading post is not open every day," he says. "Today it was open, but tomorrow it is not."

I rub at my face in frustration. Of course.

The sun is going down, and I shiver as a cool breeze sweeps over us.

"You're cold," Vrex murmurs. "I will show you my tashiv."

He strides forward and unlatches some kind of mechanism on his door. Then he gestures for me to precede him, and I step inside.

This is obviously the Agron version of a living room, and there's a pile of wood stacked next to a firepit in the corner. I glance up at the roof. It even has a cleverly constructed chimney to let out the smoke.

A few wooden chairs sit near the fire along with a pile of furs. I can see Vrex relaxing here after a long day of lumbering around doing whatever it is that huge warriors do on this planet.

"Bathing room," he says in a gruff voice, gesturing to a doorway. He strides through another door, and I trail after him, finding a large mattress sandwiched between two painstakingly carved wooden tables. I move closer, running my fingers over the top of the one closest.

"This is a dragon," I murmur.

It's gorgeous. The scales have been so intricately carved that it looks almost lifelike, and it must have taken weeks to complete. On Earth, this thing would sell for thousands.

"Did you make this?"

"Yes."

"Wow. You're seriously talented."

Vrex shifts on his feet, the first sign of discomfort I've seen from the stoic warrior. Weirdly, his awkward reaction to my compliment is kind of endearing, and I feel something in my chest relax.

"Thank you," he says gruffly. He stalks across the room

to where a huge chest sits beneath a window. My breath catches in my throat as I gaze at the view.

The water is a bright cerulean blue, the river winding between huge trees. Here and there, huge stones and boulders peek up from the water, surrounded by white froth.

"What a view," I murmur.

Vrex lifts his head from where he's using his good hand to rummage through the chest, surveying the picturesque scene in front of us. His shoulders relax as we both stand and stare at the water for a moment.

"This is why I chose this place for my home," he says.

I open my mouth—to say...I don't know what—but he's already returning his attention to the chest. He pulls out a few large furs and strides back into the living room, throwing them on top of the pile. Then he runs his gaze over my body clinically before returning to the chest and throwing a few more furs on the bed.

"I will sleep there," he says, pointing to the furs on the floor in the living room.

"Oh, you don't need to do that," I begin, but he ignores me, gesturing for me to follow him into the bathroom.

I'm treated to the same view out the window, but I'm immediately entranced by the huge tub that dominates the room. It looks like it could fit two warriors the same size as Vrex, and my skin practically itches with the need to get clean.

"Would you like to bathe?" he asks.

"More than just about anything."

He nods, and then I'm once again trailing after him as he moves back outside. A huge metal container sits next to the window, a firepit beneath it. He lights the fire and then reaches inside the window, pushing and pulling some kind of lever.

It's a pump, and I grin as water begins to flow into the bath. The grin leaves my face as I glance back up at Vrex, whose face has turned gray.

"Here, get away from that thing. I can do it. That arm needs to be in a sling."

Surprisingly, he moves out of the way, and I continue to pump the water into the bath.

"I will go check my traps," he says, and my stomach lets out a rumble at the thought of food.

His eyes are the color of good whiskey as they lighten at the sound. He hesitates.

"You will stay here," he says.

I nod, ignoring the commanding tone. I'm always pissy when I'm hurt as well.

"I'll take a bath while I wait for you."

He stares at me for one long moment. Finally, he nods and turns, ambling away.

I blow out a breath as I watch him leave. Even with the amount of pain that I know he's in, with his arm held at a ninety-degree angle, he walks with a long, easy stride, head high, shoulders back.

No, Ivy. No perving at the giant, scarred warrior.

If there's one thing I've learned, it's that "happily ever after" isn't for me. But if I'm not careful, I may end up rebounding with tall, scarred, and deadly.

I snort. The only emotion the guy has shown in my presence was a hint of frustration when he was convincing me to follow him here and a moment of grim resolve that told me he'd be throwing me onto his weird lizard creature if I didn't make the right choice. Oh, and a tiny shard of amusement when my stomach rumbled earlier.

Other than that, he's basically a robot.

Vrex

This female threatens my control.

I am under no illusion as to what my life holds. A future with a beautiful female is not for me.

I run the back of my hand along the scar that winds across my forehead. A gift from my mother's brother after she died.

Exquisite, delicate females are for other warriors. I learned young that my oversize body and clumsiness, combined with the vicious scar on my face, made the females of mating age shiver in fear.

"You will be alone," a voice hisses in my ear. *"Just like your father."*

I push Hevi's voice out of my head as I check my trap, pleased to find an udazin that succumbed to my trap recently, the beast still warm to the touch.

Truthfully, my bone aches and throbs. If I move too quickly, black spots appear in front of my eyes. I quickly butcher the udazin, thankful that I do not need to go and hunt for food today.

I'm cooking the meat when Ivy opens the door, peeking out at me. She has wrapped a fur around herself after her bath, and I attempt to wrench my eyes away from the drop of water that winds down her neck and into her cleavage.

"Do you have something I can wear?" she asks. "These pajamas are rags."

I slide the meat onto plates and nod, getting to my feet. Within moments I've found a shirt that she will be able to wear until I can return her to Rakiz. She sends me a grateful smile as I hand the shirt to her, and I wait for her by the fire.

"This looks delicious," she says as I hand her a plate.

I nod, and we eat in silence while I carefully keep my eyes off her bare legs.

"Why were your clothes so torn?" I ask finally. Her pants were little more than scraps of material, rising well above her knees.

"I thought it would help the others find us," she says, her mouth twisting. "But I'm guessing they didn't look." She raises her eyes to mine. "Thank you for helping me," she says, her voice low.

If I were an honorable male, I would tell this female that her friends did look for her. That one of them is now a tribe queen who convinced her mate to bargain with me to find her. But still I am unwilling to admit to this female that she is just another assignment. That her safety means another favor owed to me by one of the tribe kings on this planet.

This female believes that I *am* honorable. I find myself unable to destroy her illusions of me so quickly.

"Mmm, this is good," she says, and I ignore the burst of pride that her words cause. A female can sneak under a male's defenses before he is even aware of it, with her sweet words and soft skin. I've seen this happen before.

If a male is not careful, he will find himself forever changed by the female in question, without ever being truly conscious of how it happened.

"Man of few words, huh?"

I raise my head and catch the amusement in her eyes, the hint of a smirk playing around her mouth.

"I...apologize. I am unused to conversation."

Her eyes soften, and I have to look away.

"That wasn't a dig. I think most of us fantasize about escaping to a remote cabin at some point in our lives."

I nod and take another bite, not at all surprised when

the female continues talking.

"You mentioned someone who will send more warriors to help us. How do you know him?"

"He is a tribe king."

"A tribe king?"

"He rules over other Braxians. They live together in a camp."

I raise my head, and she's gazing at me curiously, obviously waiting for me to continue. I shift, and this time, I can't control my wince as the pain almost blinds me.

"We can talk later," she says. "That arm needs to be in a sling. I can help with that. I've got some training."

I nod. Truthfully, I know the bone needs to be stabilized. I get to my feet.

"I will bathe first."

Ivy

I'm a red-blooded woman.

And most red-blooded women would agree: the sound of Vrex splashing in water is a special kind of torture.

I've never been attracted to the cute guys. To the white-collar guys with soft hands and pretty mouths. Vrex, with his huge body and "don't fuck with me" attitude is about as far from one of those guys as I can get.

That doesn't mean that I'm going to do anything about it.

Just that I'm tempted.

Real tempted.

Vrex opens the door, and I swallow with an audible gulp. I can't help it. My mouth practically waters at the sight of him with his shirt off. He has the strangest blue-green pattern on his skin, across his shoulders and the top of his chest. I open my mouth to ask him about it, but my gaze is caught by the pendant hanging from a long string tied around his neck. It catches the light, the gold practically glowing in the flicker from the fire.

"That's beautiful," I murmur.

"It was my mother's. She made jewelry."

"You got your talent from her."

His chest is a work of art. His shoulders are huge, and I unashamedly let my eyes trail over his pecs, his eight-pack, and down to the *V* that points to the promised land.

He's wrapped a fur around his waist, and his arm is awkwardly held in front of him. His eyes heat as I meet them, and I feel a bolt of triumph. The robot *is* affected by me.

He's also looking even paler, pain clear on his face.

Wow, Ivy, way to perv on the injured guy.

I jump to my feet, gesturing for him to sit down. He complies, and I carefully attempt to avoid glancing down at where the fur has parted.

Jeez. Bruce and I occasionally watch rugby at his favorite Irish pub. He watches for the sport, while I unashamedly watch for the men. And Vrex has just revealed a set of huge thighs more impressive than any rugby player's.

I move into his bedroom and hunt through his chest until I find a piece of cloth that will work as a sling.

"Do you have any painkillers?"

Vrex frowns at me. "Painkillers?" he repeats in English, although the word comes out slurred as he attempts to speak my language.

"Something you can take to make it less painful?"

He shakes his head.

"Jeez," I mutter. "I'm starting to feel a whole lot of gratitude for the stuff I left behind on Earth."

"Earth?"

"That's the name of my planet," I say, stepping forward to slide the makeshift sling beneath his elbow.

He nods, his jaw hardening as I gently wrap the material around his elbow in an attempt to provide some support.

"I'm sorry," I say. "I know it hurts."

Another sharp nod.

I carefully move the ends of the material to his other shoulder.

"I just realized I never thanked you," I say.

Strangely, this makes him scowl.

"You do not need to thank me," he says.

"Dude, you saved my life. I may not like to admit it, but I was out of my depth when those giant gray tortoise guys were messing with me."

A muscle jumps in his jaw, and I stare at him.

Men. I'll never understand them.

"Anyway," I continue. "You got hurt helping me, so I just wanted to say that I really appreciate it."

Silence.

"What were you doing in that area anyway?" I ask.

His eyes glitter as he glances up at me, and I realize I'm leaning over him, my boobs basically shoved in his face as I tie the sling into place.

"Uh, that should hold. We really need to find some kind of pin for this loose bit right here, but we can figure that out in the morning. You can have the bed, by the way. You should probably sleep sitting up so you don't knock that arm."

I'm rambling, and he stares at me.

"Take the bed," he says finally, his voice hoarse. I open

my mouth to argue, and he narrows his eyes in warning.

I throw up my hands. "Anyone ever told you you're the definition of stubborn?"

He doesn't reply, and I roll my eyes.

"Fine. If you feel the need to swing your dick around, there's nothing I can do about it."

Just like that, his eyes heat, and it takes every drop of my self-control not to lower my gaze to where that fur is wrapped around his hips.

"I'll just...go get ready for bed," I mumble, and he nods.

I turn and make my way back into the bedroom. Other than the stamp of Vrex's skill on the furniture, his home has nothing that points to him being the owner. Of course, I don't expect to see framed pictures hanging from the walls, but the space is sparse and, for the most part, utilitarian.

His house is beautiful, and it wouldn't take much to make it cozy.

So now you're planning to fix up his bachelor pad?

I frown as I crawl into the bed. My eyes immediately get heavy-lidded as I pull the furs over my body.

I'm not that kinda girl. The one who leaves a toothbrush behind, and before the guy knows it, she's living with him without any kind of conversation. In fact, my commitment-phobe ways were one of the main points of contention between Steve and me.

Don't think of that asshole. He knew what he was getting into when he started dating you. You warned him for six months.

Honestly, that's what hurts the most about the whole situation. I was as up-front as possible, making it clear that I wasn't down for marriage and kids. My dad died doing the same job that I do, and I saw firsthand how it ruined our family. I was never going to put someone else through that.

But Steve thought he could change me. Men always do.

CHAPTER SIX

I vy

I wake to a knock on the door and blink my eyes open, automatically glancing to the left where my alarm would sit in my apartment in Brooklyn.

Nope, still on Agron.

"Come in," I say, and the door swings open.

"I need to visit someone," Vrex says. "You should come with me."

I blink as he disappears.

Okay.

I haul myself to my feet, staring down at the shirt he handed me last night. It's huge, but the material is thick enough that it can probably work as a dress.

Shoes may be a problem though. My feet have been ripped up after running through the forest and prexas, and while I cleaned them last night—along with the deep scratch in my thigh—I have no desire to add to my wounds.

I make my way out to the living room, where Vrex waits for me. He points at something near the fire, and I stare at the shoes.

They're not fancy—closer to a pair of flip-flops than anything else. But they'll protect my feet from sharp sticks and rocks. They also look roughly the size of my feet, which means Vrex must have made them last night or this morning.

The gesture makes the backs of my eyes sting.

"You did this for me?"

Vrex gives me an impatient look, and I almost laugh. Ask a stupid question...

"Wow, I don't know what to say."

I pick them up and examine them as I move toward one of the wooden chairs. The leather is soft and supple, roughly cut but still sturdy. The warrior made these with only one good hand.

I slide my feet into them, admiring the fit. Vrex moves closer and drops to one knee in front of me, showing me how to tie them to my feet. My mouth goes dry as he glances up at me through thick lashes.

My hand moves before I'm aware of it, pushing his hair back from his face.

He rears back, and I realize I've exposed more of his scar.

He glances away as if ashamed, and I bite my tongue. He obviously doesn't want to talk about it. Silence stretches between us, and I almost wince. I'm the most awkward version of myself with this guy.

"Thanks for these," I say finally. "I really appreciate it."

He glances at me again and nods, and I realize he hasn't spoken a single word to me yet this morning. Something tells me he's used to going multiple days at a time without talking. Maybe he used up all his words yesterday.

I smile at the thought, and his gaze drops to my lips. He stares at them for one long moment and then gets back to his feet before opening the front door.

I stand as well, feeling slightly absurd in my new outfit but grateful to no longer be wearing those filthy pajamas.

"So who are we seeing? A friend?"

Vrex stiffens. "I have no friends."

The first words he's spoken today, and it hurts my heart to hear them.

"I'm sure that's not true."

He gives me a look that suggests I'm not the sharpest knife in the drawer, and I sigh, following him out the door.

He wore his sword on his back yesterday, but thanks to his injury, he's carrying it at his hip today. Something about the way he moves tells me he's not happy about it.

I follow him into the forest, feeling like a duckling trailing after its mother. We walk for what I estimate is around half an hour, and then Vrex nods at me to stay on the path, disappearing for a few minutes.

He comes back with some kind of furry animal thrown over his good shoulder.

"Jeez, Vrex, you shouldn't be lifting that kind of stuff. Why don't you let me take it?"

He gives me a look that tells me quite plainly that that will never happen, and I roll my eyes. Then my mouth drops open as we come across another hut.

This one isn't as well built as Vrex's, but it looks like it has been in this exact place for hundreds of years. The trees are so close to the wooden walls that whoever lives here could likely lean out a window and touch them.

Unlike Vrex's home, this one has a small porch. An old man is currently sitting in a chair on that porch. He looks unsurprised to see Vrex, although his gaze trails over me curiously, lingering on the shirt I'm wearing.

The old man is large, although he doesn't come close to Vrex's size. His shoulders are slightly hunched, but his gaze is clear as he studies us. His skin is a light blue, and I count five or six sharp horns winding up from his head.

Vrex strides forward and dumps the dead animal next to the porch. The old man nods his head, and something tells me he knows better than to thank Vrex.

"This is Ilax," Vrex says gruffly. "Ilax, this is Ivy."

Ilax smiles at me, revealing sharp white teeth. "It's a pleasure to meet you."

He returns his gaze to Vrex, his eyes lingering on his sling. "I can give you something for that," he says.

Vrex shakes his head, and Ilax flicks me a look as I open my mouth to protest.

"It'd be a shame if you were unable to protect this female," he says mildly. "I have a tonic that will heal the injury in a third of the time and reduce your pain as well."

Vrex hesitates, and I keep my mouth shut. Ilax obviously knows just how to handle the stubborn warrior.

Finally, Vrex nods, although his expression is dark. I raise my eyebrow, and Ilax sends me a wink as Vrex turns to lift the animal back onto his shoulder.

"I will fix the tonic while Vrex takes care of that nasty business. Would you like to help?"

I nod, watching as Vrex disappears around the back of the house. Then I follow Ilax into his home. It's designed similarly to Vrex's house, only slightly smaller. Ilax's house has a small bedroom with a space just large enough to hold a bed, and another adjoining room filled with shelves. The shelves are crammed with herbs and plants, some of them hanging from the roof, drying upside down.

Ilax takes what looks like a mortar and pestle and grinds a few herbs before adding them to a large bowl with a splash of some kind of liquid.

"You may want to step back for this," he says, and then he adds several drops of another liquid from a wooden jar, and I gape as a thick mist rises from the bowl. I blink as my head spins, and Ilax grins at me, obviously completely unaffected.

"For the pain," he tells me. "Now for the healing."

This part takes longer, and Ilax hums absently for a few minutes. Then he glances at me, his gaze curious once more.

"Tell me," he says. "How did you meet Vrex?"

I explain my story, and Ilax nods, frowning.

"This morning, Vrex said he has no friends," I say. Ilax nods again, looking unsurprised.

"But he has you," I say, stating the obvious.

"I am, perhaps, the only one who could claim such a title. Others fear what he is, even as they use him to do the tasks they would never dirty their own hands to do. Vrex is unused to those who would call him friend. And I am just an old male near the end of my life who relies on him to keep me fed."

He winks at me, but his words ring true. I mull over this as Ilax pulls a petal off a bright-blue flower and adds it to his concoction.

"Right," he says finally, filling a cup with the tonic. "Let's amuse ourselves by watching Vrex choke this down."

It is indeed amusing to watch Vrex attempt to keep his face blank while drinking the tonic. But the lines of pain around his eyes gradually disappear over the next few minutes as we all sit on the porch.

It's incredibly peaceful here, surrounded by the sounds of the forest. Distantly, I can hear the flap of wings as a bird takes to the air. The low hum of insects and the rustle of the wind through the trees are the only other background noises, and I find myself more relaxed than I have been in days.

Tomorrow, we'll get a message to the tribe king, who'll hopefully send us some backup. Then we can go find Zoey and figure out what the hell happened to Beth.

It feels like a monumental task, and I take a moment to imagine what life would be like if all I had to do was sit on this porch and occasionally set a trap for some food.

Sure, Ivy, you'd last about three days before you got antsy.

Ilax gets to his feet and disappears into the house. From the distant sound of the water, the river is further from Ilax's house, and he keeps a large barrel of drinking water on the porch. Vrex leans over, checking the level of water in the barrel, and I suppress a smile. For all of his gruff ways, he's like a mother hen with Ilax.

The old man returns, a huge sack in his hands. He gives it to me, and I open it before frowning in confusion as I pull out a dress.

"These were my daughter's," he says, his mouth trembling for a moment before he firms it. "She was traveling with her mate when they were unlucky enough to come across a pack of Voildi."

"Are you sure we can't eat them?" Jasit's words run through my mind along with the stark hunger in his eyes as he looked at us. I flinch at the thought, and Ilax nods at me.

"The clothes are of no use to me now, and Avix would want you to have them. She was always kind to those who needed it."

I swallow around the sudden lump in my throat. "Thank you so much."

He shifts awkwardly, and Vrex gets to his feet.

"I must check my other traps," he says, and Ilax nods, glancing at me and then gesturing toward Vrex.

"Make sure he returns for that tonic tomorrow," he murmurs, and I grin.

Vrex

Ivy is quiet as we walk back to my tashiv. She refuses to let me carry the clothes, baring her teeth like a feral karja when I attempt to take the bag from her.

Strangely, I find my lips almost curving in a smile. This is surprising enough that I ponder the feeling. For the first time since my mother was alive, a female is not afraid of me.

Because she believes you to be a heroic, honorable male. What will she think when she learns that her rescue was none other than one more assignment in a long list of assignments, most of them bloodier than the last?

I scowl at the thought.

"Are you okay? How's the pain?"

I meet the female's gaze, my eyes traveling down to the shoes I made her when I woke this morning, no longer able to sleep through the pain. For some reason, I couldn't stand the thought of her delicate feet being hurt by the forest floor.

"I am fine."

She raises her eyebrow but doesn't press the subject, her head high as she gazes around us. Somehow, I know that she is attempting to memorize our route. This female may be smaller and more delicate than any Braxian female I have ever seen, but she is incredibly resilient, seemingly taking each challenge and setback she has faced in her stride.

"I was thinking," she says, and I glance at her.

"Yes?"

"Do you have a weapon I can borrow?"

This female continues to surprise me at every turn.

"You would like a weapon? Do you believe I cannot protect you?"

She sends me a look as if I'm behaving like an unreasonable child. "No. You sure kicked ass when we were in the prexas. But it'd make me feel safer if I had a weapon too."

I consider this. "A sword this size will be too unwieldy. However, I do have a large knife that could work."

She nods, grinning at me, and I have to look away from her sparkling eyes. They're an interesting color—not green and not brown, but they seem to change depending on the light.

My tashiv appears through the trees, and I lead Ivy inside before opening the large chest near my fire.

"Whoa," she murmurs, staring down at the weapons. "Are you preparing for a war or something?"

I shrug my good shoulder. "Do you have any experience with fighting?" I ask, shifting a crossbow aside as I search for the long knife I had in mind for her.

"I have a black belt in karate. That's a martial art on Earth," she says. "Let's just say that I'm quick on my feet but I've never actually fought for my life before. At least, I hadn't until I got to this planet."

Her mouth twists slightly, and I find that I don't like seeing her eyes dim.

"You were obviously successful if you managed to escape a pack of Voildi," I say, and I'm rewarded with her grin.

I hand her the knife. "If you're quick on your feet, this should be a good weapon for you."

She smiles, taking the knife from my hand. "Thanks."

She should look ridiculous, her fiery hair clean but still tangled—I forgot to give her a comb, I realize—while dressed in nothing but my shirt, which swallows her, even as she clutches the large knife in her hand.

Instead, she looks strangely endearing, her smile inviting me to smile back.

I don't. Instead, I lean down and take her mouth with mine.

The shock of need is instant, hitting me like a punch to the gut. It slams into me, taking over, until I want nothing more than to strip my shirt off her body, to run my mouth over every inch of her creamy skin.

My blood pounds in my ears like thunder as Ivy lets out a broken moan, her hands coming up to clutch at my shoulders, her mouth softening under mine.

I want her desperately. And it's the craving for her, the sheer *need*, that makes me pull my mouth from hers, makes me frown as I look down into her eyes, blurred with pleasure.

This brave, kind female is not for me.

"This is a mistake," I say. Her eyes clear, the expression on her face cooling as she steps back. My hands instantly fist as I force myself not to reach for her.

She doesn't protest. Instead, she simply turns and walks away.

Ivy

I manage to bully Vrex into returning to Ilax the next morning. He seems amused by my nagging, and we walk over to his neighbor's tashiv as soon as we've eaten a quick breakfast of fruit.

Ilax seems pleased to see me wearing one of his daughter's tunics with a pair of soft leggings underneath, although his eyes turn sad for a moment as he stares at me.

"You combed your hair," he says finally, and I grin at him.

"I sure did. It was so difficult that I was about ready to hack at it with my knife."

Vrex whips his head to glare at me, seemingly scandalized at the thought, and I burst out laughing.

After he's finished his tonic, we make our way back to his tashiv and stay just long enough for him to saddle up Nari. I may be imagining it, but it seems like he's in less pain today, and he seems to be moving easier as well.

He climbs up onto the mishua and then reaches down, clasping my arm with his good hand. The breath escapes my lungs with a whoosh as I'm suddenly sitting up in front of him.

God, the guy is strong.

With him sitting behind me, his good arm wrapped around my waist, I'm exceedingly aware of the fact that he hasn't tried to kiss me again.

"This is a mistake."

I mean, he's not *wrong*, but that doesn't mean I don't feel a little rejected. What woman wouldn't after a guy kissed the daylights out of her only to immediately turn cold as ice?

I scowl at the thought.

It's probably close to an hour before we arrive at the

trading post. The sun has only been up for a couple of hours, and the clearing is busy with all kinds of aliens tempting me into gawking.

Of course, *I'm* the alien here, and they gawk back before quickly glancing away when their gazes move behind me to Vrex.

His muscles got tenser and tenser as we approached the trading post, and now it seems like he's almost vibrating with tension.

I glance over my shoulder at him, blinking as I come face-to-face with a scowl that dares the receiver to approach him.

No wonder everyone seems so scared of him.

"Assassin of Agron," I hear a woman murmur, and I narrow my eyes at her. She looks like she could be related to Ilax, with the same-colored skin and similar horns rising from her head. She quickly glances away, and I can practically feel Vrex's mood get darker behind me.

The trading post is little more than a few tashivs, sitting behind ten or twelve stalls where vendors are selling everything from meat and fruit to scrolls of paper. Vrex jumps off Nari, and I know for a fact that the pain from the movement must have made him want to throw up, but his face stays completely blank.

He attempted to remove the sling before we left his tashiv. But I refused to get onto the mishua unless he wore it. Our standoff finally ended with him giving me a dark look before muttering to himself as he mounted Nari.

God forbid the guy show any hint of weakness.

Now his expression is like stone as I jump down beside him. He ties Nari to a tree, and then I trail behind him as he heads straight for the smallest tashiv on the left. I'm so busy glancing around at the stalls and the wares that it takes me a moment to notice that everyone has suddenly gone silent.

I turn, scanning the small clearing. Every single alien is looking at Vrex, and their faces are filled with fear. As if the guy is suddenly going to start slaughtering everyone in sight.

Suddenly, I'm completely, unreasonably offended.

"What are you all looking at?" I hiss. "Take a fucking picture; it'll last longer."

Most of them turn away, although a few of them stare back at me. I'm not the most threatening person on this planet. I have no claws and no horns, and I'm shorter than most of the oversize people here. From the look on one guy's face, he's unimpressed by what he sees.

Vrex is a few steps in front of me and glances over his shoulder, raising one eyebrow. His eyes have turned that whiskey color that tells me he's amused, and he turns his gaze to the gawkers behind me. Suddenly, people have better things to do than stare at us.

"I am beginning to think that your personality reflects your fiery hair," Vrex murmurs as we step into the tashiv. I send him a look, and his mouth twitches. "Ferocious female."

This tashiv is just one large room, with what looks like a smaller room attached to it. A man with deep-green-colored skin steps out of the smaller room, a piece of paper clutched in each of his four arms.

"Vrex," he murmurs. Even this guy, who obviously knows Vrex, seems wary of him. Vrex nods and hands him a piece of paper before turning to go.

I frown. "That's it?"

"Yes. We will return in two days to see if Rakiz has returned my message."

Rakiz. I haven't heard the tribe king's name before, but I tuck it away for future reference. Getting information from Vrex is like pulling teeth.

"I have something to show you," Vrex says as we leave the tashiv. No one stares at him when he's facing them, all of them keeping their attention firmly on their own business. I rub at my chest, attempting to ease the squeezing sensation that I feel while witnessing the way Vrex is treated by these people.

He's been nothing but good to me, and they treat him like he's a dangerous monster.

"Oh yeah?" I feel the weirdest urge to reach out and take his good hand in mine, but I push it away. Vrex is ignoring the people around us as we walk back to his mishua, and I attempt to do the same.

He nods. "It is not far from here and won't take long with the mishua."

"Sure." I shrug. "Let's go."

CHAPTER SEVEN

I vy

"Asshole," I mutter as Nari pushes past yet another branch, and Vrex has to reach out with his good hand to stop it from hitting me in the face. Nari snorts like she understands me.

"We're almost there."

If I didn't know better, I'd think that was amusement in Vrex's voice.

"You know, I'm like a fish out of water on your planet," I tell him. "I'd love to see how well you'd do on Earth." I snort at the thought. Once everyone got over the sheer size of him, they'd probably try to convince him to be a male model. He's not pretty, but once you look at his hard face and those whiskey-colored eyes, it's a challenge to look away.

"Tell me about your planet," he murmurs.

"Well...it's nothing like this one, that's for sure. At least where I live. Men don't carry around swords, and you don't have to worry about potentially being attacked by a pack of flesh-eating cannibals at any moment. Although, we have to deal with door-to-door salespeople, which is basically the same."

He grunts behind me, and I laugh.

"You know, I blame the Arcav for this. We had no problems before they invaded, looking for their mates. Once they'd found the Arcav queen, they left Arcav bases across the planet, saying they were there to protect us from the Grivath." I scoff at that. "In reality, I think they were there to make sure we humans didn't get any ideas about kicking them off our planet. Life kind of returned to normal after they invaded, believe it or not. Unless the blood test found that you were a match as an Arcav mate. But it was still a small portion of the population."

Vrex is tense behind me. "What is a blood test?"

I explain how it works. "Every living being has what we call DNA. One of the Arcav scientists had a meltdown when his mate died, and he was responsible for messing with human DNA. Now human women have to get their blood tested to see if they're a match and an Arcav mate."

"Are you a match?" Vrex's voice is hard, and his arm tightens around my waist.

"Nope. Don't get me wrong, I would've been open to checking out another planet one day. Arcavia sounds awesome—their technology is way ahead of ours. But I was pretty damn happy that I wouldn't be expected to give up my career and move to Arcavia. That's kind of ironic now, huh?"

I grimace at the thought of the Grivath. I thought the Arcav were assholes when they invaded, but at least they *pretended* to play nice with us.

Vrex is silent for a long moment. "What is a 'career'?"

"It's different for everyone. I'm a firefighter." I describe my work, and Vrex pulls Nari to a stop, staring at me when I turn around to see what's going on.

"You run into buildings that are aflame?" His eyes move to my hair, and I laugh.

"I wear a ton of protection, and it's not like I do it alone. We're putting out the fire to save people's lives."

"What would make you do such a thing?"

I attempt to ignore his tone. From the way Vrex has described this planet, it's clear that women don't really get out much.

"My dad was a firefighter. He went down in the twin towers. He was a hero, and I always wanted to be just like him." I turn back around, staring sightlessly at the trail in front of us as Nari begins walking again. "When my mom found out I was going to be a firefighter... Let's just say it didn't go well. She was broken by my father's death, and she always hated that he was constantly putting his life in danger. When I finally admitted that I was planning to do the same thing, she told me not to contact her again until I'd changed my mind. She moved down to Florida with her boyfriend a year later, and I haven't talked to her since."

I ignore the way my eyes sting at the thought. Who knows if I'll ever get the chance to talk to her again?

"I'm sorry," Vrex murmurs in my ear, his tone grave.

"Thanks. It is what it is, I guess. She didn't have it in her to spend any more time wondering if a family member was going to come home, and I'd dreamed of being a firefighter since my dad let me try on his helmet when I was six."

"It is...difficult when parents behave this way," he rumbles, and I open my mouth to ask him about the pain in his voice, but the mishua breaks through the trees, and my mouth drops open.

"Holy shit. It's our ship."

I can feel Vrex nod behind me. "I thought you might want to look at it."

I glance over my shoulder at him. "I do. You're a good guy, Vrex."

His cheekbones turn a dull red, and I grin.

"Are you blushing?"

"No," he grinds out. "Go see it before I change my mind."

I laugh at him as I jump off the mishua before shifting from foot to foot while he ties Nari to a tree branch. He reaches into one of his packs for a handful of food for her, giving her a pat on the snout while I wait impatiently.

Then he joins me, and we both stare at the ship. If it were a car on Earth, my dad would've called it a "write-off."

"How the fuck did we survive that?" I murmur. Vrex tenses beside me, glancing from the crumpled visage of the ship to my body and back again. He seems to be thinking the same thing because his face is grim, his body tense as we move closer.

When I stumbled out of this ship with the other women, the purple aliens who bought us were all dead. Not all of them had died on impact. From the blood splatter, it was evident that the aliens who had survived the crash had then been taken by surprise by the pack of Voildi. Those Voildi pretended to be our rescuers and convinced us to follow them. In reality, they were taking us home for dinner. And we were going to be the main course.

The door is still flung open, and I brace myself for the stench of decomposing corpses. But they're gone.

"What happened to the bodies?" I mutter, glancing at Vrex. He shrugs and obviously immediately regrets it, his mouth tightening as he winces. Just a couple of days ago, he refused to let me see his pain, and something unclenches in my chest as his face clears.

Small steps.

Get it together, Ivy. Quit stalling and check out this ship.

I move closer to the ship, Vrex shadowing my every move. When I attempt to stride up the stairs, he hauls me back before drawing his sword and stalking up the stairs in front of me.

I don't stick my foot out and trip him for being an over-protective alpha male, but it's a close call.

Vrex's shoulders relax when he reaches the top of the stairs, but he keeps his sword in his hand. I follow him inside, and he steps out of the way, revealing the ravaged control center of the ship.

There may not be any bodies, but there's still plenty of blood. It stains the floor, the walls, and the huge window, which must be near indestructible, since it seems to have bent with the force of the crash instead of breaking.

I wrench my gaze away from the rust-colored stains. Those assholes got what they deserved. I walk down the metal stairs to the room where we were kept after we were loaded onto this ship.

Vrex is silent beside me while I stare at the cage.

"It still doesn't seem real," I murmur. "I know it happened. But sometimes I still need to pinch myself so I know I'm not dreaming. That we were taken for no reason at all." I glance at him. "What makes people think that they can treat others this way?"

His body is tense next to me, his eyes narrowed in fury as he stares at the cage. I think this is the most emotion I've ever seen from him, and it's his rage that pulls me from my pity party.

"Come on," I say. "I want to make sure I've seen everything."

A few minutes later, I find it. Something that makes my

mouth dry, makes my hands shake. Next to one of the broken monitors, a red light flashes every few seconds. For some reason, that red light raises every hair on the back of my neck, and I run my palms along my forearms in an attempt to get rid of the goose bumps.

"Hand me that sword, big guy."

Vrex attempts to hand it to me, then grabs it back as I almost drop it.

"How the hell do you carry that thing around so easily? I'm pretty damn strong for a woman. Never mind. I need you to smash the shit out of that light."

Vrex shrugs and slams the hilt of his sword into the control panel. He scowls as we both watch the light continue to flash red. He hits it again and again, denting the control panel and smashing the monitor, but the light itself doesn't stop flickering.

"Shit."

"What is it?" Vrex asks.

"I don't know. It could be nothing, but if I were in charge of a bunch of spaceships like these, I'd make sure they had some kind of locating device in them. This entire ship is toast, but this one thing is still working. It freaks me out."

Vrex nods, glowering at the light.

"Well," I say finally, "there's nothing we can do about it now. Maybe when I find the others, we can all come back and try to figure it out. Thanks for bringing me here today. It helps to see this."

Vrex meets my gaze, his jaw tight. Finally, he nods again. "You're welcome."

Vrex

"Like this?"

I nod as Ivy sets the trap. She is a fast learner. When she insisted that I teach her how to set traps for protection and to catch food, I was surprised. But with her shoulders set in determination, she has adjusted one of my favorite traps so that it is now more easily hidden—and likely more lethal.

"Where did you learn to do this?"

Her voice is sad. "My dad was big into the outdoors. He wasn't a prepper or anything, just liked to teach me what he knew." She looks up with a small smile. "When you're that young, your parents are still your heroes. I lost my dad when I was eight, so while I know in my head that he was just a man with flaws like any other, in my heart he's still superhuman."

I nod, and she looks up at me from where she's crouched on the ground.

"Do you see your parents often?"

I tense. "No. We should go back to the trading post after we have seen Ilax. It is likely that there will be a message waiting for me."

Her eyes search my face at the change of subject, but she nods, brushing the dirt off her hands as she stands.

"Listen," she says. "I wanted to thank you again for everything you've done. It's nice to know there are men on this planet who are willing to actually help us, you know?"

Guilt stabs through me like a knife. I open my mouth to tell her the truth—that I'm not her hero, I'm just another mercenary profiting off her and her friends. But her smile is so broad, her eyes sparkling as she peers up at me.

"You're welcome," I say, my voice thick.

I saddle my mishua while Ivy carefully watches my

movements. She seems determined to learn as much as she can about this planet, and for some reason, this makes me rub at my chest.

We're silent as we make our way to Ilax, and she grins at him as we find him sitting in his usual spot outside his tashiv.

My arm is much better, and I will soon be able to remove the sling. Ilax nods and hands me the tonic while we watch Ivy sneak the mishua a handful of food from her pocket.

"She is different, this human," Ilax murmurs.

I nod, handing him back the cup. "She is."

"And you? Will you keep her?"

My mouth drops open, and the old male laughs.

"Is it such a crazy question?"

"A female like this is not for me."

Ilax sighs, his expression softening. "I do not understand why you insist on thinking this way."

"You are just like your father. A useless waste of space. You will always be alone. Always."

I attempt to push Hevi's words aside, but they still ring true.

I can feel Ilax's eyes on me as I watch Ivy pat Nari on the snout. She laughs as the mishua ducks her head, demanding more attention.

Ilax sighs again. "You are an honorable male, Vrex. I'm sorry that you do not believe yourself worthy of a mate."

He is wrong about my honor, but I don't bother arguing, staying silent until he shakes his head, muttering to himself as he moves back into his tashiv.

Ivy leaves the mishua, the sun glinting off her scarlet hair as she moves toward me, her lips still curled in a grin.

"We should go," I tell her, and she raises her eyebrow.

"Okay, let me just say goodbye to Ilax."

I ready the mishua while she says her goodbye, and the old male steps back out of his tashiv with her.

"Think about what I said," he calls to me, and I nod, waving to him after I pull Ivy up onto the mishua.

"What's he talking about?" Ivy asks.

Ilax narrows his eyes at me and then shakes his head as if declaring me too stupid to live. Then he waves us off dismissively, stomping back into his tashiv.

"Nothing," I say.

Ivy's quiet on the way to the trading post, and I frown at the back of her head, used to her easygoing chatter. By the time we arrive, the trading post is busy, darkening my mood further.

I tie the mishua and follow Ivy, who moves straight toward the messenger tashiv, ignoring the many eyes on us.

I grit my teeth, finding it difficult to do the same. Usually, I am able to easily ignore the terror in the locals' eyes as they look at me. But when I am with this human female, I feel ashamed that I am a creature that so many fear.

The messenger tashiv is busy when we arrive, but those who are waiting quickly move aside as I step through the door.

I grind my teeth until Ivy winks at me.

"Man, that would be a really helpful skill to have on Earth. I'd never have to wait in line again."

I feel my lips curl, and her eyes widen.

"Strange female."

Color creeps up her cheeks, and I stare, entranced, until the Taxu steps forward, clearing his throat. He hands me a piece of paper, and I glance down.

"These are not from Rakiz," I say. Ivy's face falls, and I guide her out of the tashiv, attempting to ignore the way I want to pull her close. How I want to take her mouth again and hear her soft sighs as she opens for me.

"Who are they from?"

"Another tribe king. He has a task for me."

I scrawl a message back, telling Thane that I am currently completing another assignment. I glance at Ivy, my stomach twisting.

She climbs up onto the mishua while I stalk back into the tashiv, and she's once again quiet when I mount behind her.

"Can I trust you, Vrex?" she finally murmurs.

I tense, and Nari throws her head in response.

"You cannot trust anyone on this planet," I tell her finally, my voice hard. "You would be wise to remember this."

***

Ivy

We clomp slowly along the forest path, both of us silent. I don't know what Vrex is keeping from me, but from the tortured expression on his face, he's not happy about it either.

Even after his warning, I *do* trust him. I trust him to keep me safe, to help me find my friends, and to not hurt me.

Maybe that makes me an idiot.

I frown. "What the hell is that?"

Nari freezes in place, and Vrex jumps off his mishua, his boots hitting the ground with a thump.

"Stay here," he orders me, and I watch as he moves closer to one of his traps. Nari follows him until he turns around and glowers at her and she freezes in place.

Now that we're closer, I can see exactly what's caught in Vrex's trap.

It's a Voildi.

He's impaled by one of the huge sticks that Vrex is constantly sharpening, and he's writhing on the ground in front of us, clearly in agony.

Bile rises, and I'm about to turn away when the Voildi glances past Vrex to me.

"You," he chokes out. "I knew you were here."

I don't recognize this Voildi, but God knows there were enough of them in the pack that stole us.

I stay silent, and he laughs.

"The Zinta has paid for you, female. He will keep searching until you are his."

Vrex leans forward, blocking my view of the Voildi. The forest suddenly seems loud, birds chattering, animals scampering. Something is happening.

"How many of you are here?" Vrex demands.

"Vrex," I say. He holds up a hand, and the Voildi laughs again, his yellow face turning the color of sour milk.

"Hand her over," the Voildi advises him. "This is just the beginning."

"Vrex! I smell smoke."

He turns to me, inhaling deeply, and his expression is suddenly so agonized that I struggle to take a deep breath.

Vrex leans down and swipes his sword along the Voildi's throat, and then he's sprinting toward me before landing on the back of the mishua and urging her forward. He wraps his good arm around me, holding tight as the mishua lurches through the forest toward Ilax's tashiv.

It's already in flames when we arrive.

We jump off the mishua and sprint toward the tashiv.

"Wait!" I scream at Vrex. I grab a couple of blankets from

Ilax's chair on the porch and shove them into the barrel of water. I hand one of the dripping blankets to Vrex and wrap the other one around my shoulders and head.

"Stay here," he orders me. I ignore that, following him in just a few steps so I can see where he's going. If this tashiv collapses, someone's going to have to help them both get out.

"Oh God."

It's the back room that's on fire. The one with all Ilax's healing tonics. Ilax is lying in the main room, bleeding out from a wound in his chest. Vrex throws me a furious look as I follow him in, but he lets me help him get Ilax out of the tashiv.

He places Ilax on the grass and leans over him, his face desperate. "What do you need? Which tonic?"

"It's too late for that, boy."

Vrex ignores him, picking up the huge barrel of water and heading back into the tashiv.

I stare after him, torn, and Ilax grabs for my tunic. "He will be back. Look after him for me."

I lean over him, finding the source of the bleeding. Someone has stabbed him, likely with a fucking sword, given how huge this wound is. I pull the blanket off my shoulders and push against his chest.

"You're going to be okay," I tell him, and he laughs.

"You are as bad as he is."

A roar of fury sounds from the tashiv, and then Vrex is back, falling to his knees next to Ilax.

"Your tonics are gone," he says, his face hard. "I know another healer. You just have to stay with us until I can get you to her."

Ilax ignores that, reaching his hand out to Vrex. Vrex

takes it, and I have to glance away. I can barely swallow around the lump in my throat.

"They'll be coming back for her," he warns, glancing at me.

"This is my fault," I murmur. "I'm so sorry."

He shakes his head, wincing at the movement. "Not your fault. The innocent are never at fault when evil comes for them." He turns to Vrex and raises an eyebrow. "A lesson some of us are slow to learn, hmm?"

I choke out a laugh. Even while bleeding out, Ilax is still attempting to lecture Vrex.

Vrex's eyebrows draw together, and he gestures for the mishua.

"No." Ilax's voice is firm. "I am a healer. I will not make it, boy. I will die here, surrounded by my forest. And then I will join my family. They are waiting for me." He turns to me. "He will blame himself for this. Do not let him. Be patient with him."

I nod, and then he gasps, his face contorting with pain. Vrex's eyes are wild as he glances back toward Nari, but Ilax squeezes his hand.

"Thank you for looking after an old male in the last years of his life. Your mother would be proud."

Ilax chokes, blood running from his mouth. But he smiles as he looks up—through the canopy of trees in his forest, to the emerald sky...and beyond.

CHAPTER EIGHT

I vy

We bury Ilax in his forest, close to the porch where he spent his days. Tears run silently down my face as Vrex digs the grave, refusing to let me help as he works one-handed.

If not for me, Ilax would still be sitting on that porch, staring out at the trees, waiting for Vrex to visit.

Vrex is silent until he has finished filling the grave. We managed to put out the fire before it could spread through the forest, but Ilax's tashiv is mostly gone.

They must have been watching us to know where to hurt us the most. This is a warning, but if they think I'm going to hand myself over to them, they're wrong.

This is war.

Vrex obviously agrees because his face is hard as stone as he turns to me.

"They will all die for this," he says. He strides toward the mishua and helps me back on. Even Nari seems depressed, her head low as we slowly plod back toward Vrex's tashiv.

We find two more Voildi in Vrex's traps. One of them is already dead, and the second is unconscious. I look away as Vrex leans down and kills the Voildi without even getting off Nari's back.

He instructs me to wait on the mishua while he examines the other traps around his home. Then he checks the tashiv itself before he returns for me.

"It's safe," he mutters, and I jump down so he can unsaddle Nari.

I hover awkwardly near him. "Can I help?"

He shakes his head, and I move inside, giving him space.

I pace for hours. Vrex seems to be compulsively checking his traps, disappearing in different directions only to return a few minutes later.

I simultaneously want him to join me and yet don't know what to say to him. There's nothing *to* say. I came to this planet, he helped me, and I got his only friend killed.

The guilt is crushing. It rips into me, shredding my insides as I watch the huge man secure his territory. His face is as hard as ever, but his eyes...

I look away, absently wiping my hands on my tunic. They come away sticky, and I stare down at the blood staining them.

Ilax's blood.

I spin as the door opens, and Vrex steps inside. His gaze drops to my hands, and I almost hide them behind my back like a child.

"They'll pay" is all he says.

I nod. "We'll make them pay."

"Tomorrow we leave. We will check for any messages

from Rakiz. If there are none, then we go to him. It's no longer safe here."

I flinch, and he narrows his eyes on me.

"You think I can't protect you?"

I shake my head. "No. I'm sorry your territory was invaded."

"It was only a matter of time. You should get ready for bed. We will sleep early."

I study his face. His expression is blank, and he holds his shoulders straight, his head high. But somehow, I know he's barely holding it together. When he falls apart, he's not going to want me to see it.

I nod and head to the bathroom, where I quickly bathe. I wrap a long fur around my body when I'm done and move toward the bedroom. Vrex is sitting, staring at the unlit fire, but I hear him enter the bathroom as I pull on my clothes.

I lie awake for hours, tossing and turning. Finally, I get up, planning to sneak past Vrex to grab some water.

He's awake though, still sitting in the same chair, ignoring the furs near the fire. He glances at me, pain stark on his face.

I can't help it. I walk over to him, reaching out. I don't know for what. He catches my hand and pulls me to him, plundering my mouth.

His lips turn gentle, and he stares at me with dark eyes as I raise a shaking hand, running it over his cheek.

"You shouldn't be alone tonight. Come sleep in your own bed."

He doesn't argue, following me into his room. I pull the furs over us as he hauls me close, his huge hand cupping the back of my head.

"He was a good male," he says suddenly, his voice hoarse with grief. "When I first decided to move here, I was a young warrior, my voice still breaking. He taught me how to grow vegetables."

I try to blink back my tears, but they spill from my eyes and onto his neck. "I'm sorry."

"It's not your fault. It's mine. I should have known he would be a target. I should have convinced him to let me set more traps around his tashiv."

"It's not your fault either. He was a stubborn man."

"He was." Vrex is quiet for a long moment. "Go to sleep."

Neither of us truly sleep. I nod off occasionally, then wake as Vrex's body tenses below mine. At one point, I reach up and find his face wet. He tenses further, and I shush him.

"It's okay to mourn your friend."

He's silent, and I pretend to sleep, giving him privacy as he grieves.

***

Ivy

I wake to a hot mouth on mine, and I gasp, a moan leaving my throat as Vrex's lips travel to my neck. It's still dark, but in spite of how tired I am, I'm desperate for him, my skin too tight, my thighs trembling.

He kisses me right below my ear, and my hands clutch at his shoulders.

"How are you so beautiful?" he murmurs.

I smile in the dark. "I could ask you the same thing."

He snorts and then kisses his way down to my breasts. My tunic is gone, I realize.

"Did you undress me?"

He pauses, raising his head. "I may have helped you out of your clothes."

"Jeez, I must've been really out of it."

"Large animals make less noise when they sleep," he agrees solemnly, and I laugh.

He returns his attention to my breasts, a low curse leaving him as I shiver at his attention, my nipples hardening. He takes one of my nipples in his mouth, flicking his tongue against it, and I sigh, trembling against him.

The muscles in his back flex as I run my hands over them, and I dampen further. His body is insane.

I move one of my hands around, running my fingers along the hills and valleys of his abs. He lifts his head, his jaw tight as he catches my hand in his.

"It has been too long. I may embarrass myself if you touch me right now."

I smile at that, and he curses, dropping a kiss to my lips. We make out for a few minutes until I'm writhing against him, and he lets out a low laugh at my impatience.

I feel drunk when he kisses me, and I immediately want his mouth back when it leaves mine. But he's moving down my body, kissing and nipping and *licking*.

He hums against my thigh, gazing up at me, and the image of him between my legs makes me gasp.

I'm aching for him. His fingers dip into the wet heat of me, stroking and playing while I writhe. His head lowers, and this time I'm the one cursing as he slides his tongue over the sensitive bud of my clit.

"Inside me," I say, my voice hoarse. "Now."

He glowers up at me as if I've taken away his favorite toy, but from the hard line of his jaw, I can tell he's barely holding on to his control.

I want him to lose it.

His thick shaft presses into me slowly, and his head lowers once more as he plunders my mouth. I groan against his lips as he thrusts all the way in, right where I'm aching for him.

He thrusts again and again, driving me crazy as he grinds against me. He reaches his hand under my butt, angling my hips, and my eyes almost roll into my head as I wrap my legs around his waist.

My climax hits me, and I gasp as he buries his head in my neck, continuing his relentless, skillful rhythm. He drives himself into me, and incredibly, I feel another climax burning up my spine, my body shuddering as I cling to him.

I open my eyes, finding him gazing down at me, something like reverence in his eyes. He quakes above me, rocking into me once more as he lets out a low groan.

We're silent for a long time. I don't know about him, but I feel shell-shocked, wrung out by the pleasure that just exploded through me.

He hauls me on top of him, and I don't miss the stark pain on his face as he uses his bad arm.

"You need to be careful with that," I tell him breathlessly, and he raises his eyebrow. It's evident that he's not used to anyone caring, and my chest tightens at the thought.

"Why do you live out here all alone, Vrex? Don't get me wrong, it's beautiful, but you keep mentioning the camps that your people live in."

He's quiet for a few moments. "I used to be a member of Dexar's tribe. He is another tribe king, only this was when his father was still ruling. My mother died while attempting to bring my sibling into this world. She had always been weak, prone to sickness, and she lost too much blood."

"I'm so sorry."

He stares up at the ceiling, his fingers running through my hair. "When she died, my father fell apart. He turned to noptri—a drink that steals your wits," he explains at my frown. "Suddenly, he no longer cared that he still had a son." His voice hardens. "I take after my mother. I have her eyes and many of the same features. My father could not stand to look at me."

My heart breaks at the pain in his voice. He was just a kid who'd lost his mom. His father should have been there for him.

"So what happened?"

"He gave me to my father's brother. They already had sons and wanted no more, but his mate had been close to my mother, so she agreed to raise me."

"I'm guessing that wasn't a good thing."

His jaw hardens, and I lift my hand, running my fingers over his cheek. He glances back at me, and something seems to soften in his eyes.

"Now that I am fully grown and I can look back, I believe there was something broken in my uncle. Something wrong with his mind. He would tell me that I was just like my father. That I would grow up to be alone, just like him. He would beat me, tell me I was useless, that my father lost himself in noptri to forget about his failure of a son."

My hands shake as I sit up. "Where is this asshole now?"

My fury seems to amuse Vrex, and the corner of his mouth twitches as he pulls me back down to him. "Dead. He challenged the wrong warrior from another tribe and was sliced apart."

"Good," I growl. "Why didn't the tribe king help you?"

He shrugs. "The qatai's health was failing. Not many people knew, of course, but I was sometimes close to Dexar. His father was also obsessed with growing the tribe and taking down any who threatened the safety of the tribe."

"What about Dexar? He could've done something."

"I wanted nothing more than to leave the tribe. As soon

as his father died, I petitioned Dexar, and he allowed me to leave."

Vrex strokes his finger down the line between my eyebrows as I scowl.

"So he never helped solve the problem? He just let you walk away?"

"That *was* solving the problem," Vrex says gently. "I prefer to be alone."

I ignore the hurt that slices through me at that. People who abuse children are very good at convincing those children that it's *their fault*. It sounds like both Vrex's father and uncle taught him that if he let people close to him, they'd fail him, or worse, abuse him.

"Your uncle should have paid for what he did."

"A few years later, I found out that he had attempted to seduce my mother before she mated with my father. I believe he had convinced himself that he was in love with her and that my father took her from him. When she died, I was a living memory that she chose another male."

I grind my teeth at that. "I don't blame you for leaving. I would've told all of them to go fuck themselves and left the tribe as well."

He huffs out a breath, his fingers returning to play with my hair. "I have no doubt that you would have, little Flame Hair."

I attempt to ignore the way my toes curl at his low voice. "You know, you act like you're no good with women. But from what I've seen, you're chivalrous, kind, and one hell of a good lay."

Vrex is silent for a long moment, his fingers gently untangling my hair. "Females are frightened of me," he says matter-of-factly. I study his face, but his expression is completely blank.

"I don't understand why," I murmur.

"You are a brave female," he says. "You are never afraid of me, even when you should be. Most females do not like my size. They have heard of my...reputation, and *this* disgusts them." He reaches up a hand, pushing his hair off his face so I can see his scar.

I snort, and he narrows his eyes at me, obviously confused. Most of the time, I forget his scar is even there.

"You can't be serious."

He tilts his head.

"About the scar thing. I can *maybe* understand the other stuff, although they sound like little bitches to me. But the scar is hot."

I've managed to shock the warrior. He stares at me as if I've suddenly announced that I'm planning to take off my clothes and ride his mishua through the forest.

"Hot?" His voice is strangled, and I frown at him.

"Come on, the whole tortured soul thing? The remote cabin in the woods, the air of mystery, the seven feet of pure delicious male, and then the interesting scar? If you were on Earth, you'd be snapped up in a heartbeat."

He glowers at me, rolling away. "You are mocking me."

I blink at him. "I'm not."

"People on this planet know me as nothing more than the Assassin of Agron. The only females who deign to lie with me are those who care more for my coin than my reputation."

"You pay for sex?"

He blinks at me, as if surprised that *this* is what I've latched onto. "Did you hear nothing of what I said?"

I wave that away. "Yeah, yeah, you're a fearsome warrior, a misunderstood male, yada yada. But who do you pay for sex?" Yup. I sound jealous.

Vrex gives me a scathing look. "Whores in Sebe who are willing to overlook the scar on my face in return for a few orgasms and some credits."

He's trying to shock me with his words, but it doesn't work. Instead, I slide one leg over him until I'm sitting up, staring down into his grumpy face.

His eyes are hard, his jaw tight. And he won't even look at me.

I sigh and lean down, pushing his hair away. He tenses, his hands rising to my shoulders.

"Shh," I whisper. "Let me."

He closes his eyes, and his huge body trembles as I gently kiss every inch of his scar. When I'm done, his eyes are dark, unfathomable, and blazing with need as he rolls me onto my back.

He spends the rest of the night dragging moans of pleasure from my lips.

I'm still tired in the morning, but I smile as Vrex nuzzles me awake.

"We must go," he says. "I have packed what we need, and we can eat on the way."

I blink up at him. "Okay. Just give me a few minutes."

It doesn't take me much longer than that because he's already packed my clothes. The clothes that Ilax gave me.

My chest tightens at the thought, but I picture the peaceful expression on his face as he stared up at the sky and thought of his family. I hope he's with them now.

Vrex slides my knife into a sheath, which he fastens around my upper thigh, on top of my slim pants but beneath the tunic. If I need to reach for it, I'll lose time pulling up the tunic, but I should still have the element of surprise.

Vrex has removed his sling, and his arm doesn't seem to

pain him much as he leads us along a new trail. When I ask why we're traveling in a different direction, he informs me that he spent the early hours of the morning setting even more traps. Anyone who attempts to get close to his home will regret it.

For once, there aren't that many people at the trading post when we arrive. Vrex leads me into the messenger tashiv, and the guy who works there instantly hands him a couple pieces of paper.

We walk back to the mishua, and I watch him as he reads the first note. Finally, I sidle up close to him, wishing I could understand the language he's reading.

My eyes widen. Beneath the first note is a second message. And it's written in English. I don't hesitate, leaning forward to pluck the piece of paper from Vrex's hands.

"Hey, Ivy, this is Nevada," I read aloud. Vrex tenses, and I frown as I continue, "If you get this, congrats on that whole staying alive thing. We've hired this hulking piece of man-meat to help you get back to us. Zoey and Beth are fine, so if you want to get off this planet, you need to start moseying toward our camp."

I look up at Vrex, betrayal hitting me like a punch to the gut.

"How much?" I demand.

"How much what?"

"How much are you getting paid to bring me back?"

He's silent for a long moment. "Two hundred credits and a favor from the tribe king."

"A favor?"

One sharp nod. "Ivy—"

I lift my hand. "Why didn't you tell me? You let me think you were helping me just because you happened to be in the area."

Vrex's jaw tightens, the look in his eyes strangely desperate. He turns his head, and I realize everyone is staring at us.

"We need to leave," he says, and a harsh laugh escapes me. Even now, he can't explain himself. I crumple the note in my fist and then flatten it out before carefully folding it and sliding it into the pocket of my tunic so I can read it again later.

I get on the mishua and try to ignore the wrenching pain in my chest. "Fine."

CHAPTER NINE

V rex

Ivy is as cold as ice as we travel toward Rakiz's camp. I'm planning to leave her with the tribe king and then hunt the Zintas and the Voildi once she is safe.

I should have told her. Should have admitted that I was sent to help her. I can't explain why I didn't. Except that for a brief period, I wasn't just the Assassin of Agron. I was the male who saved the human female with the flame-colored hair.

I wanted to be more than just a killer. More than just a mercenary. For her.

"Will you not talk to me now, female?"

She sniffs. "I need some time, Vrex. I'm pissed at you."

I attempt to ignore the way my shoulders straighten with hope that she will forgive me. Last night was the best night of my life.

A night that should not have happened. I am not worthy

of the flame-haired female with the wide smile and sparkling eyes. But for a few short hours, she was mine.

I'm not ready to give that up.

"I did not think you would be the type of female to punish me by withholding your words," I tell her, and she inhales sharply, glowering at me over her shoulder.

"You *deserve* the silent treatment," she snaps. "You let me think that you just so happened to be close by and you decided to help me because you were a *good man*."

I tense, hoping she can't see how much her words sting.

"You are an honorable male, Vrex. I'm sorry that you do not believe yourself worthy of a mate."

I scowl as Ilax's words run through my head on a loop. The male was wrong.

"That was your first mistake, little Flame Hair. Believing that I was *good*. I warned you not to trust anyone on this planet."

She shakes her head in disgust as she turns back around to face our trail. "You're right. I should've listened."

I grind my teeth in frustration. "If you want me to be your villain, I can," I say, and she stiffens.

"Is that a threat?"

"No. I'm merely willing to conform to your expectations of me."

I lean forward and run my teeth down her neck. I'm rewarded with her gasp even as she curses at me.

I grin with my lips pressed against her skin. "You still want me."

She leans back and elbows me in the ribs. "I still want chocolate, but I don't seem to have much of that in my life right now."

I frown. What is this "chocolate"? And how will I find it for her?

We are close to the edge of the forest, and I turn Nari toward the plains that will lead us to Rakiz's camp. Already, I feel tense at the thought of being surrounded by so many people. But it is the idea of leaving this female behind that makes me itch beneath my skin.

A huge tree is lying across our path, and I pull the mishua to a stop.

"Can we go around it?" Ivy asks.

My instincts are roaring at me. "I don't like the look of this. Stay on the mishua."

She nods, and I jump down, drawing my sword. I approach the felled tree slowly, noting that there have been no recent storms. There are no other fallen trees in this area.

I turn. "We will find another route."

A Voildi drops out of a tree, and I growl. I'm suddenly surrounded.

"GO!" I roar at Ivy. I whistle at the mishua, and she turns, racing back through the forest, Ivy holding on tight. The Voildi curse, a few of them giving chase while the rest of them attack.

***

Ivy

Five minutes after declaring himself a villain, Vrex made his mishua take me to safety while surrounded by a pack of Voildi.

I don't think so.

Now I'm hiding in a bush after bailing from the mishua, who was running through the forest like her ass was on fire.

I creep back toward the Voildi. Vrex is swinging his sword like a wild man, but there are too many of them.

I run through options in my mind. If I had a gun, I could take them all out. Unfortunately, all I have is a large knife, and while I'd probably do okay up against one Voildi, I'd be sure to die if I attempted to take on them all.

They're going to kill him.

I flinch as Vrex's giant sword slides through one of the Voildi just as another one darts forward and slices his own sword along Vrex's side. Vrex roars, whirling around and beheading the guy, but another is quick to replace him, slashing his sword across Vrex's ribs.

I sprint toward them.

Vrex swings his arm, the sunlight glinting off his sword as he smoothly steps away from the Voildi, sliding under his guard and cutting his head off his shoulders. He lifts his own head, baring his teeth at me in fury.

Yeah, yeah, I didn't listen. Sue me.

I leap into the air, landing on the back of one of the Voildi and driving him into the ground. I slam the back of my knife into his head, and he doesn't get up.

"Move," Vrex roars, and I glance behind me, my mouth going dry at the sound of hooves thundering on the ground as Nari charges toward us. I roll aside, and she lowers her head like a bull, driving into the fray. Her horns pierce and stab, while Vrex takes advantage of the chaos, swinging his sword like he's possessed.

I jump to my feet, and then I'm falling as my foot gets caught on something. I try to get up, but whatever has me isn't letting go, and I flip onto my back, staring at a Voildi who holds the rope that's tied tightly around my ankle.

A trap. And I fell for it.

I try to crawl away, a frustrated sob leaving my throat as he laughs, stepping closer.

"Ivy!" Vrex's voice is thick with what sounds like panic.

And then everything goes black.

Vrex

The world turns red as I slash my sword across a Voildi's throat and blood sprays across my face. The creature slashes at me with its sword, and I duck, kicking out as I turn, plunging my own sword into its gut.

The Voildi thought it could sneak up behind me. That I wouldn't smell its stench as it approached.

I shy left, ducking as another Voildi swings, and cut across its arm, the limb falling to the ground. It screams, and I ignore it, turning my head as I frantically search for Ivy.

The flame-haired female is quiet. Too quiet.

A Voildi leaps at my back, the tip of its knife carving through my shirt and into my shoulder. I spin, slicing as it falls, and it collapses, blood pouring from its throat.

There. Ivy is fighting with a Voildi. He has her ankle caught in a rope on the edge of the clearing, and I roar her name as he leans over, picking up a rock before slamming it into her head. She instantly goes limp, and I barely dodge a blade as it slices toward me. I fight to get to her, but the Voildi disappears with her slumped over his shoulder, melting into the trees with several of his pack members.

Another Voildi lunges desperately at me, and I crouch, slicing along its thigh. I move as he falls before stomping on the back of his neck.

I pant, wiping blood off my face.

Nari steps close, lowering her head and almost poking me in my eye with one of her horns as she attempts to nuzzle me.

I stroke her nose before pushing her gently away.

I count eight Voildi already dead, but one of them is twitching. I stalk over to him, and his face pales.

"Where did they take her?"

"To the Zintas. Don't kill me. Please."

I ignore that. This Voildi would have laughed as I was slaughtered and likely eaten my body.

"Where?"

He begins to babble, and I put a picture together. We are close to the Colossal Water. The Zintas traveled here from across the water, and if they take Ivy with them, I may never see her again.

"Don't kill me," he begs again.

I return my attention to the Voildi, raising an eyebrow as blood bubbles between his lips. And then I run my eyes over the huge wound in his chest.

"I don't need to."

Nari clomps toward me, then nudges me with her nose.

"Yes," I say. "We're going to find her. Now."

Ivy

When I pictured Vrex rescuing me, I imagined it happening *before* I ended up on a rickety, shabby boat.

It looks like a bunch of logs have been tied together and a hut built on top. What it doesn't look like is a seaworthy vessel. Even if the Zintas *did* use it to cross the water to get here.

"Nuh-uh," I say, but the Zintas ignore me as they drag me closer to the boat, and small rocks and stones shift beneath my feet as I struggle.

I'm no match for the two Zintas holding me, each with a hand clamped around one of my arms. The waves lap against the shore, and the sound would be relaxing if I weren't staring at a small vessel that looks like it's guaranteed to flip or sink. I'm a strong swimmer, but who even knows what creatures are waiting for me beneath the water on this planet?

I shiver as my imagination presents all kinds of scary beasts, with tentacles and sharp teeth, waiting to drag me into the depths below.

What if Vrex is dead? What if those Voildi managed to kill him and he's lying somewhere in the forest?

Or what if he killed them and decided I'd brought enough pain and heartache to his life? And then he headed back to his cabin in the woods?

"That was your first mistake, little Flame Hair. Believing that I was good. I warned you not to trust anyone on this planet."

I shiver. Surely he wouldn't leave me. Right?

I stop struggling as the Zintas turn so that I'm facing the hill, and I scowl at Aroth as he slowly makes his way down the grassy incline.

"You have cost me a lot of credits and time," he says once he's a few feet away. "When the Voildi did not bring you to me as agreed, I went to their lair and killed many of them until they swore they would fulfill their side of the bargain."

I sneer at him. "You'd think you'd see it as a sign that you should move on with your life. This will end badly for you."

Aroth laughs. "You know what I like about you, Flame Hair?" I flinch at the reminder of Vrex's nickname for me, and Aroth reaches out to touch my hair.

I jerk my head back, and he laughs again.

"Your species is weak. You have no weapons and are smaller than most of our children. And yet you talk as if you are stronger and faster than all of us combined. Fascinating."

Yeah, yeah, I have a big mouth. Since he enjoys it so much, I clamp it shut, glaring at him. He lowers his head, studying me from beneath thick eyebrows. "We have not seen creatures like you on our side of the Colossal Water. You will provide wealth for our children's children's children."

I bite my tongue. *"Pretend inferiority and encourage his arrogance."* I can see my dad, sitting next to my bed and grinning at me above his book. He'd expect me to be smart about this.

Aroth seems to lose interest, turning away and ordering his men to get ready.

Where are you, Vrex?

I still have my knife, but I'm not an idiot. I'm not going to be able to take down all of these guys with a knife shorter than their forearms.

"He will win who knows when to fight and when not to fight."

I just have to hold on. Vrex will find me, and in the meantime, I'll wait for my chance. They've already proven that they underestimate me.

"He will win who, prepared himself, waits to take the enemy unprepared."

I study the Zintas' every movement as they throw wooden boxes onto the boat. They pull up the anchor, and then they're gesturing us forward.

I dig in my heels, but one of the Zintas just picks me up, holding me in front of him with his arms wrapped around me, trapping my arms down by my sides.

My throat feels like it's closing up as my heart races. I really don't want to get on that decrepit boat. In fact, I'm coming perilously close to begging.

The Zinta passes me up onto the boat and sits down before placing me next to him, his hand clamped around my upper arm tightly enough to bruise. My gaze flicks from the boat to the rocky shore, to the Zintas, and back again as I concoct and discard one escape attempt after another.

"Move," one of the Zintas suddenly roars, and I turn my head as Aroth strides through the shallow water and climbs onto the boat. My heart stops as I gaze up the hill to where Vrex is sitting on Nari, his sword in his hand as she gallops down the hill, feet scrambling for purchase on the stones.

I punch the Zinta holding me in the face, and he growls, reaching to grab my free arm. His hand is like a vise wrapped around my bicep, and he simply pulls me closer as I kick out at him.

"Ivy!"

We're pulling away from the shore, but determination is clear on Vrex's face as he jumps from Nari's back and sprints toward us.

Aroth turns from where he's sitting at the end of the boat and screams at his men, who paddle faster. Vrex splashes through the water, teeth bared as his eyes lock on my face.

Aroth kicks one of his men off the boat, then reaches out and pushes another one into the water.

"Kill him," he demands.

The Zintas splash into the water, and we're now deep enough that it's almost up to their chests. Aroth doesn't expect them to kill Vrex, I realize. He's just hoping they'll slow him down long enough for us to get out of here.

Vrex kills the Zintas in the blink of an eye, but it's still too late. He roars, the anguish clear on his face as he attempts to get to our boat only to sink beneath the water.

He flounders, and terror makes my mouth dry. He can't swim.

"Stop, Vrex! Please!" I beg as he comes up, gasping for air. He's going to drown, but he doesn't listen, and I choke on a sob as Aroth screams louder at his men and we float further and further away.

CHAPTER TEN

Vrex

I...failed.

Of course you did, my uncle sneers in my head. *Did you expect otherwise?*

No. I just need to get across this water. I know no one with this ability. But that does not mean that I can't find someone.

Ivy is a survivor. If there is one thing I've learned about my little Flame Hair, it's that she will never give up.

The Zintas may think that they have won. But Ivy will fight. And when I find her, they will wish they had never been born.

I haul myself onto Nari's back, and she charges up the hill. We travel for hours until we're finally approaching Rakiz's camp. Nari is exhausted, and I feel half dead, desperate for water, by the time I arrive.

Rakiz's sentry stops me before I get close enough to see the camp walls.

"I need to see Rakiz," I tell him. "He owes me a favor."

The sentry's eyes widen as he realizes who I am, and then he nods, allowing me to pass. This is repeated with four more sentries, and I raise my eyebrows as I find Rakiz waiting for me.

"Your security is impressive," I say as he crosses his arms, leaning against the camp wall as if he could not care less that I have arrived with no warning. The look in his eyes is hard, however.

"My queen insisted that we make some...adjustments," he says, and his eyes warm as the female—Nevada—approaches. He wraps his arm around her and nods as my eyes drop to the slight bump of her stomach.

"We have been blessed by the gods," he says softly, sliding his hand along her stomach.

She elbows him with a laugh. "That's one way to put it. I wasn't feeling all that blessed when I couldn't eat my breakfast this morning."

Her tone is light, but it's obvious that the tribe king and queen are filled with joy. Envy hits me like a punch to the gut.

"Congratulations."

"Thanks," Nevada says as Rakiz nods at me. "Sooo, where's Ivy?"

"That's why I'm here. I need help."

Rakiz stares at me for a moment, openmouthed. "I had never thought I would hear those words from your lips," he says.

"I never imagined I would say them."

Rakiz gestures for one of his men to take Nari to eat and

rest, and then I follow him and Nevada to their tashiv, ignoring the eyes on me.

The female who steps into the main room stares at me curiously, and Nevada smiles at her.

"Arana, would you mind bringing some food and water for our...guest?"

She nods and sends me a smile, and Rakiz gestures for me to sit before being seated himself. He pulls Nevada close, and she sits on his knee, resting her head against his as she gazes at me.

"Is Ivy okay?" she asks, her voice serious.

"She has been taken." I almost choke on the last word, getting to my feet to pace.

"Why don't you tell us what happened?"

I feel time running through my fingers like water. Where is Ivy now? Is she okay? Are they hurting her?

"Vrex." Rakiz interrupts my thoughts. "Start at the beginning. When did you find Ivy?"

I race through the events of the past days, stumbling over Ilax's murder. I push away the memory of the hurt look in my little Flame Hair's eyes when she learned that I had been sent to find her.

I will find her once more. And then I will never lose her again.

Distantly, I realize that I am falling apart. My hands clench and unclench as I tell Rakiz of the Zintas and the contraption they used to cross the Colossal Water.

"They had a boat?" Nevada gets to her feet. "How did I not know that people had boats on this planet?"

Rakiz reaches for her hand, stroking his thumb along her palm. "I know of one male who has attempted to build similar contraptions," he says to me. "But he is a member of Thane's tribe."

"Thane? His camp is not near the Colossal Water."

"No, but Thane has given this male permission to live next to the Colossal Water while still being under the protection of his tribe. He is hoping to be able to cross the Colossal Water and trade, just as the Zintas have been doing."

I nod. "We must leave."

Rakiz raises one eyebrow. "We?"

I nod again. "I am calling in my favors."

"Which favors?"

I narrow my eyes at him. What use are my favors if my little Flame Hair is in danger?

"All of them."

***

Ivy

I stare at the town in front of me as the Zintas drag the boat onto the shore.

And it *is* a town. The buildings are several stories high in places, and while some are similar to the wooden buildings in Sebe, many of them also seem to be made from some kind of brick.

We only sailed for a few hours, so I'm assuming that we've either crossed a lake or traveled from the tip of one continent to another. But wherever we are now, it's different from anywhere I've been on Agron so far.

The Zinta grabs me, pulling me onto the shore, and I survey the dock a few hundred feet away. A larger boat—one similar to what I've seen in fishing villages on Earth—is currently docking. An alien with four arms steps forward to help with a fishing net.

I blink, stunned. It makes sense, of course. Even on Earth, some countries are more developed than others. But I'm still struck by the hustle and bustle of this place compared to the area where our spaceship crashed.

"Move, human." The Zinta pulls me after him, and I whip my head from side to side as we leave the dock and they practically drag me through the town. Several Zintas stay behind and begin unloading the boat, and I scan the area. I need to get back here and steal that boat at the first opportunity.

The Zintas seem more relaxed here, although they travel in a tight pack, their voices low as they joke with one another.

We walk down a narrow street, and I stare at the people around me. They're living their lives, not at all surprised to see a group of Zintas "escorting" a strange alien woman through the streets. I lock eyes with a woman who looks similar to a Braxian female, only she has purple skin. Her brow lowers as she sends me a sympathetic look, and then she skedaddles out of the way before she's pushed aside.

A few minutes later, one of the Zintas moves ahead and unlocks a huge wooden door. It swings open, and my eyes slowly adjust to the dim light.

Inside, the building is larger than it appeared from outside. Most of the Zintas disappear through a door to the left, while Aroth gestures to the Zinta holding me.

"Clean her up and then put her in the hole. We will sell her tomorrow."

I grind my teeth, wishing I could wipe the smug look off the furry bastard's face.

Patience, Ivy. Wait for the right time.

The Zinta drags me into what I'm assuming passes for a bathroom. "Wait here."

I use the facilities while he leaves, locking the door behind him. When he returns with a bucket of water and a small rag, I wipe my face and limbs, unwilling to take off my clothes while he's watching.

He seems unconcerned, and he simply reaches out when I'm finished. I flinch as his hand wraps around my arm once again. That arm is going to be covered in bruises.

He leads me through another room, which is currently empty, but from the low armchairs, it seems like some kind of living room. I raise my eyebrow as he opens a door, and then he's dragging me toward a hole in the ground.

A heavy metal grate sits next to it, with a bunch of huge rocks likely used to keep the grate in place.

Oh, hell no.

I forget about my plan to pretend to be compliant. I forget about waiting for the right moment and not letting them see I can fight.

I forget everything as I stare at the hole. I elbow the Zinta in the face, following it up with a kick to the balls as he folds.

Huge arms come around me, picking me up like I'm a sack of flour.

"Enough," Aroth growls. "You will either hold onto the rope and be lowered down or I will throw you down and listen to your bones as they snap."

I freeze. My tunic is riding up, and if I'm not careful, these guys will see the knife I've worked so hard to hide.

My eyes dart, but I'm surrounded.

"Fine," I croak out, and Aroth gestures to the Zinta that was holding me.

"Get the rope."

My eyes sting as they lower me down, but I won't let them see me cry. I let go of the rope when I'm on the ground, and they pull it up before slamming the metal grate closed.

I stare up at the grate as their footsteps fade away. I'm guessing I'm about twelve or thirteen feet down, and from the look of the smooth walls, getting out of here is going to be a bitch.

I sit on a rock, which has been pushed up against the wall. There's a rust-colored stain on one half of it, and I can't even let myself think about who else has been held down here and what happened to them.

I feel painfully, achingly alone, and I let my head fall back against the wall as I picture the look of retribution on Vrex's face as he struggled to get to me. He came for me. He would've gotten to me too if they'd taken just a little longer to load that boat.

"You deserve the silent treatment," I told him. *"You let me think that you just so happened to be close by, and you decided to help me because you were a* good man.*"*

What is *wrong* with me?

Vrex didn't deserve that. Even if he was sent to find me, he still saved me, still helped me over and over again. I wasn't mad because he was sent for me. I was mad because he didn't tell me. Because I wanted to be someone he *wanted* to be around. Just like he is for me.

He *is* a good man. The kind of man who looks after an old man in the forest. The kind of man who makes shoes for a stranger because her feet are cut up. And the kind of man who almost drowned attempting to save me on the shore.

I've been abducted, kidnapped, and kidnapped again. By now, it's likely that I've lost my career, and this planet has been one near-death experience after another. But amongst all the heartache and fear, I've known that as long as Vrex is around, I'll be okay.

And as soon as I find a way out of this hole, I'm going to tell him that myself.

Vrex

It takes longer than I would like for messengers to travel to the tribe kings who owe me favors. I manage to sleep for a few hours but wake when my arms reach for Ivy to pull her close.

By the time the sun has risen, I'm pacing the kradi, and as soon as I hear the camp come to life, I head back to Rakiz's tashiv.

He meets me outside. "Thane has replied. He's more than happy to give you access to his subject in return for owing you one less favor."

I nod, relief hitting me in a rush. "I will go there now."

Rakiz examines me. "We will go with you. Dexar has also replied, and he says he knows of Thane's water-obsessed subject and his location. He will meet us there."

I nod. "Thank you."

All this time, I thought I was saving my favors as leverage. That they would ensure that I could be left to live my life alone. But fate had other ideas. I was saving them so that I could use them to rescue my little Flame Hair.

Although, I will not be at all surprised if she has already freed herself and is waiting on the shore across the Colossal Water, tapping one of her small feet impatiently.

My lips curl slightly at the thought, and Rakiz raises one eyebrow. He opens his mouth, but the door to his tashiv opens, Nevada striding out.

"I'm coming with you."

From the look on Rakiz's face, this is the last thing he wants, and I turn away, watching as Rakiz's warriors saddle their mishua for the trip to the Colossal Water.

Nevada and Rakiz are hissing at each other in low voices, but from the sound of Rakiz's deep sigh and Nevada's throaty laugh, it's evident that she has won their argument.

I turn back as Rakiz growls. "You will not place yourself in danger at any time."

Nevada nods, taking his hand and placing it over her lower stomach. "I'd never risk our baby," she murmurs. "But I want to be there for Ivy too."

I glance away, unwilling to break up their intimate moment. I think of our plan, considering all the things that could go wrong.

The entire plan hinges on the actions of one reportedly insane male who lives close to the Colossal Water.

"We are ready," Rakiz says, drawing me from my thoughts. "Let's go find your female."

CHAPTER ELEVEN

I vy

I shiver in the hole all night. After hours of attempting to keep myself warm and after I almost go hoarse screaming that I need the bathroom, the Zintas finally drop down a rope. I'm hoping that I'll get an opportunity to escape, but the same Zinta who attended me earlier wraps his huge hand around my arm as soon as the rope clears the top of the hole. He escorts me to the tiny, windowless room that passes as a bathroom before locking me inside while I do my business.

I use the same bucket of water to wash my hands and then I search for anything I can use for a weapon.

"Ivy. Ivy. *Ivy.*"

My mouth drops open as the sound of clashing reaches my ears. Someone is roaring, and I pound on the door, slamming my fists against it as I attempt to break it down.

"Vrex?"

The door opens, but it's the Zinta who grabs me and pulls me through the large sitting room, which is now covered in blood. Red stains the floor and the walls, and I twist in the Zinta's hold, almost tripping over multiple bodies along the way. The Zinta hauls me back outside, and I freeze.

"Vrex!"

They have him surrounded, and he lunges toward me. The scuffle is short, but within moments, they're pushing him down the hole, and I choke out a sob as I hear him land with a muffled groan.

The Zinta hands me the rope while Aroth stalks toward me.

"Get down there before I push you down. The warrior will soften your fall."

I'd rather be stuck in a dark hole in the ground with Vrex than up here with these motherfuckers. The Zinta lowers me down while Aroth roars at his people, obviously enraged that Vrex was able to follow me here and do so much damage. But I block it all out as soon as I'm lowered enough that Vrex can pull me down into his arms.

I stare up at him, furious even though his battered, swollen face is the best thing I've ever seen.

"What were you thinking?" I snap.

"I couldn't leave you here alone."

I wrestle with that for a moment. This wasn't a breakout attempt?

"You got put in here on purpose?"

He grins at me. "I couldn't get you out without first getting *in*. And I've killed enough of them that they need to regroup."

I sigh, reaching up to prod at my head. Fireworks explode in front of my eyes as my fingers brush over the bump, and Vrex leans forward, catching my hand. The Voildi knocked me out when I was taken, and I'd give just about anything for a few painkillers.

"You know, for a self-confessed villain, you seem to care a lot about the woman you were hired to find."

His jaw tightens.

"You should have left me. Why would you do something so stupid?"

"I couldn't leave you."

"Well, now they have both of us to keep each other in line. They'll threaten me to make you behave. And as soon as they sell me, they'll kill you."

"That's not the fighting spirit I'm used to."

I glare at him, and he holds me close while turning his head to examine our surroundings.

If I were going to trap two people in a hole in the ground, I'd definitely design it just like this. The walls are made of smooth stone, and while I'm pretty good at climbing, I doubt I'd be able to scramble up to the top without risking a nasty fall.

And if Vrex tried to climb it and slipped? His huge body would crush me.

It's suddenly silent above us. "Where do you think they've gone?" I whisper.

"Likely to arrange for your sale."

I grit my teeth at the thought. "Are you okay?"

He nods. "Get on my shoulders."

"Huh?"

He crouches, and I sigh but climb on until I'm sitting on him like a kid at Disney World. Then he slowly rises to his feet, his huge hands wrapped around my knees to help me balance. I see where this is going.

I'm tall enough to reach the grate, and I push my hands up against it. "Shit."

It's not budging. My guess is that they've reinforced it with those rocks now that Vrex is in here with me.

Vrex crouches back down, and I climb off his shoulders as I blow out a breath.

"Well, the good news? They can't force us to come out. If they try and come down here, we can kill them." I hand Vrex the knife from beneath my tunic. His mouth drops open, and I nod at his frown.

"Yeah, women are continually underestimated. On all planets. The problem is that they'll eventually just starve us out. If they withhold water, we'll be begging them to let us out of here."

I slump down, suddenly depressed, and Vrex leans over, taking my chin in his hand.

"I swear to you, no matter what happens, I will come for you. I will never let them take you away from me, not while I still have breath in my body."

He brushes away a tear as it falls down my cheek, and then I'm burying my face in his chest as he wraps his arms around me, stroking my back.

"It's been one hell of a week," I sob, and he murmurs his agreement.

When my face feels hot and swollen and I've got no tears left, I slowly move back. "We need to come up with some kind of plan."

He nods. "We will respond based on their actions. Let's see what they do."

I blow out a breath. "Okay." We're quiet for a long moment, and then I sit on a large rock, leaning back against the wall.

"I'm sorry," I say. "I shouldn't have yelled at you when I

found that note from Ivy. It's just...my ex lied a lot. We just broke up, and I think I'm still dealing with it."

"He lied to you?"

I nod. "He wasn't trying to be hurtful. He wasn't cheating on me or anything. It was little things. He'd say it was fine that I had to cover a shift or that I'd probably miss dinner. He said he knew what he was getting into when he first asked me out. If he'd just been honest, maybe we could've worked it out, or I could've broken it off earlier before we got to such a bad place. It turns out that it was never fine. He decided I didn't care about our relationship and broke up with me on the phone. By distance," I clarify, when Vrex's face is blank. "He wasn't with me, but we were talking."

Vrex looks intrigued, and for a moment I fantasize about what it would be like to take him back to Earth with me.

He's silent for a moment, and then he frowns. "I should be apologizing to you. I'm sorry that I didn't tell you Rakiz had sent me to look for you."

"Why didn't you?"

He shifts, obviously uncomfortable. "You were the first female I had met who was not afraid of me. My only skills are hunting and killing. I had nothing to offer you, and you...joked with me. You talked to me like I was just a warrior. I'm used to everyone else believing that I am nothing but the Assassin of Agron. But with you...it was different. I didn't want to lose that."

My heart cracks. "You're good at a lot more than just hunting and killing, Vrex. I've seen the furniture you carved in your home, and you're incredibly talented. You're funny when you let yourself relax. You're amazing in bed. You're kind and caring, and you made me feel safe, even when I was lost on a strange planet. I know it was your uncle who made you think you were a monster. But even living life as an assassin couldn't turn you into the monster he called you."

Vrex's eyes darken as he stares at me for one long moment and then reaches for me, wrapping me in his arms again.

I snuggle close. "Why do you collect favors? What do you use them for?"

He shrugs, leaning his chin on the top of my head. "They're security in this world. A guarantee that I'll be left alone."

I nestle closer to him. "Is being alone really that great?" I feel as if I'm asking myself the same question, and we're both quiet for a long moment.

"I thought so," he murmurs, running his chin gently along the top of my head. "But now I'm not so sure."

I smile up at him, and he leans down, pressing a kiss to my forehead.

"I have used my favors to get across the Colossal Water. And I will use the rest of them if it means that you will be safe. Don't worry, little Flame Hair. I won't let them hurt you."

I blink back tears. "You used your favors for me?"

He nods. "Rakiz has spread the word. Anyone who owes me a favor has been notified that I need help."

I thought I had no tears left, but more of them are winding hot trails down my face.

"I'll help you get new favors," I promise, and he grins at me, his white teeth flashing in the low light.

"I don't need favors...if I have you."

Ivy

A few more hours pass before a Zinta appears, leering down at us through the grate. "Stay seated if you want this water," he warns. "If you get to your feet, I will pour it on you."

Vrex vibrates with fury next to me, and I reach for his hand. Both of us want nothing more than to take this guy out, but we have no idea how many other Zintas are out of sight above us.

Earlier, Vrex handed me back my knife and instructed me to hide it. But we need to wait for our chance.

We stay seated, and the Zinta lowers a bucket of water on a rope. I'm thirsty, but I wait until the Zinta has replaced the metal grate and walked away before I turn to Vrex.

"Do you think it's drugged?"

He shrugs. "If they drug us, they will need to climb down here and pull us up."

I reach out a hand and scoop up some water, tasting it. Vrex watches me closely.

"I will wait before I drink some," he says. "If you become unconscious, I will at least be able to fight them off. If we both are unconscious..."

"We're screwed."

He nods, and we spend a few minutes in silence. His hand clenches occasionally, as if he's missing his sword.

"This is a terrible, horrible, no good, very bad day," I mutter.

He glances at me.

"My favorite book as a kid. Never mind. We need to start thinking about a plan. Want to hear my thoughts?"

Vrex narrows his eyes at me, and I have the weirdest feeling that he's reading my mind.

"They're going to take me, Vrex. And when they do,

you're going to lose your shit, and they're probably going to kill you. Not only are we seriously outnumbered, but you don't even have your sword."

"I won't let them take you."

"Listen to me—"

"No."

"Vrex."

He narrows his eyes at me, lowering his head as his chin sticks out stubbornly. God, his mom must have had her hands full with him when he was a kid.

"I need you to find me," I say, getting to my feet. I grind my teeth as he stares at me silently. I need to speak his language.

"You're no good to me dead," I snap. "I need you to play along, let me be taken, and then you can break yourself out of here."

He growls, reaching out and snagging my wrist. "And what if I can't get to you in time? What if my favors don't come through?"

"Trust me to stay alive. If those furry guys are planning to sell me, that means they don't want me dead. At least not right away. I can look after myself. So let me do it."

I stare down into his hard face, and then I'm pushing his hair back and running my finger down his long scar.

"One mark of a great soldier is that he fights on his own terms or not at all," I quote. He stares at me, frowning, and I brush my fingers over his cheek. "I trust you to find me," I whisper. "Trust me too."

He trembles for a long moment, and then he pulls me closer, pressing his lips to mine. He kisses me like I'm something infinitely precious. Like he can't handle the thought of losing me. Like he'll come for me, no matter how far they take me.

"I don't want to lose you," he murmurs. "I just found you, little Flame Hair."

"We've got this," I reassure him even as my heart pounds at the thought of being separated from him. This is the best plan, I know it. If they take me to be sold, they're unlikely to be focused on Vrex for a while. I shiver. At least I hope so. I'm trying to ignore the little voice in my head that tells me they'll kill him when they take me.

No. After the way he killed so many of them and with his reputation on this planet, they'll want to kill him slowly. Bile rises, but I know I'm right. They'll want to make a spectacle of his death.

I tremble harder at the thought. What if he doesn't escape? What if they take me and then kill him and I never see my huge, brave warrior again?

How did it come to this? How did I end up feeling so much for this guy in such a short time? After I'd spent my life holding people at a distance, Vrex kicked down my walls, stalked over my boundaries, and made me care more than I'd ever thought possible.

"I can't lose you," I murmur. "Please don't let them kill you."

He shakes against me, and I glance up. "Are you...laughing?"

"I may not agree with your plan, Ivy, but it is a good one. Their attention will be split, and they will believe me wounded and unable to get free from here."

I glance up at the metal grate holding us prisoner. "And how *will* you get free from here?"

He smiles, and my breath catches in my throat as I stare at him.

The smile leaves his face as we're both silent for a long moment, and I raise my hand, running my finger over his lips. "You're even better looking when you smile," I mutter. "You shouldn't do that when there are any other women around. Ever."

His eyes widen, surprise flashing over his face, and then he laughs. "You think any other female would amuse me like you do? Besides, other females are afraid of me, remember?"

His lips twist, and I grin at him. By now, I know him well enough to be sure that the blank expression he's slapped on his face is covering up the hurt.

"Good," I say. "Keep being scary. I don't want to have to fight any bitches for my man."

The breath leaves him, and he stares at me like he's never seen me before.

I raise my eyebrow. "What?"

He smiles again, and my chest clenches.

"Yeah, I was serious about you not doing that around anyone else. Keep that sexy smile for me," I joke.

"You are the only one who makes me want to smile," he says. Then he leans back slightly and reaches behind his neck. "I want you to wear this," he says, tying the necklace around my neck.

"Vrex...I can't. This was your mom's."

He nods. "She would have loved you," he says. "This symbol is for protection. It will keep you safe until I can find you."

I swallow around the lump in my throat and stroke the gold pendant as Vrex pulls me into his arms and kisses me again.

"We're going to make them pay," I murmur. "Them and the Voildi. For what they did to Ilax and for what they've done to us."

He nods. "We will."

Vrex

The moment that they take Ivy from me is one of the worst of my life. It's as bad as when I learned that my mother had died. As bad as the day my father sent me away. And as bad as the moment I found Ilax in a pool of his own blood.

It takes all of my self-control to stay seated as they lower a rope and instruct her to hold onto it.

"We've got this, Vrex," she murmurs. Her face is pale, her lower lip trembling, but she squares her shoulders. I clench my fists, battling the urge to reach for her, to take her lips with mine. We've already said our goodbyes and agreed to this plan.

But it is not easy.

She takes the rope, and I want to roar as she's lifted above me. Panic makes my hands shake, and I sit on them, determined to keep my promise, knowing that Ivy is right, that we must be separated for a short time.

But the voice in my head urges me to pull her back to me. To not let her out of my sight. To not risk *her*.

"Remember your promise," Ivy murmurs, her eyes holding mine. "Wait for the right time and then fuck some shit up."

My lips are numb. "I promise."

I pace the small space like an animal when the metal grate is pushed back into place. This is what I have avoided. When I am foolish enough to get close to people, they are taken from me.

But I will get her back.

I strain, focusing all my attention on listening to what the Zintas are doing above me. It's quieter than it has been, and it is likely that most of them have gone to deal with whoever they are selling Ivy to. It's unlikely that they would want to risk being outnumbered while selling her. Otherwise, the buyers may simply kill the Zintas and take her from them.

The grate is still in place, but I reach for Ivy's knife, hidden behind the rock she was sitting on not long ago.

"They'll find it on me," she said, running her hands over my chest as I shook my head, unwilling to take her weapon. "We had a deal, remember? You need to get out of here."

Finally, I agreed, finding no other way to be able to scale the walls of this cage.

The walls are smooth, but there are still plenty of notches between the rocks for me to bury my knife. I shove the blade deep into the wall above me, using it for leverage. And then I begin to climb. My feet slide and sweat runs down my face as I painstakingly use the knife to make my way up the wall, focused only on getting to Ivy.

"I trust you to find me. Trust me too."

I am unused to trusting anyone and even less used to being someone who is trusted. But I will not fail her.

I finally reach the grate. I lift one arm out to push against it, clinging to the knife with my other hand, my body shaking as my boots scramble for any kind of leverage.

I shove as much weight as I can into the grate, and surprisingly, it lifts. I blink sweat out of my eyes, using all of my strength to flip it up.

Rakiz's laughing eyes meet mine.

He reaches down, and I lunge for his arm, hauling myself up and flipping onto my back, panting as I stare up at the roof for a few moments. My bad arm howls at me, but I roll to my feet, narrowing my eyes.

"What are you doing here?" I snarl, glancing around. I can hear the Zintas in another room, somewhere above us.

"I couldn't risk a full-scale attack in case they killed you. I had a feeling that would negate the spirit of the favor I owe you."

"You look much too amused by this."

"I have to say, rescuing the Assassin of Agron from a cage across the Colossal Water will be a story that few will believe."

"Where have they taken Ivy?"

"Dexar is following her with his men. He wants to wait and attack all the Zintas along with anyone who thinks to purchase a human woman. He has become obsessed with the safety of his human qatal, and he says it will send a signal to anyone who would consider harming her."

My mouth drops open, but we both clamp our mouths shut at a movement above us. A Zinta roars with laughter, and I turn my attention back to Rakiz.

"Dexar is here?"

"Of course. You think he would miss the chance to remove one of the favors he owes you?"

I blink at that.

"Are you two finished having your little catch-up? Or would you like some tea and cookies while you gossip?" a voice hisses, and I turn my head to see Nevada crouched by the door, half hidden in the shadows.

I gape at Rakiz. "You brought your queen *here?*"

"She refused to stay with the boat. Besides"—Rakiz's face turns cold, death in his eyes—"I will slaughter anyone who thinks to touch her."

"I can hear you," Nevada mutters. "And in case you forgot, I can do the slaughtering myself."

Rakiz leans closer to me. "She is acting as something she

calls 'lookout.' She has promised to leave before we attack." He turns his head. "Haven't you, karja?"

"Yeah, yeah." Nevada's voice is sulky, but I can see her stroke her hand over the slight bump of her stomach. "I'm outta here. Have fun." She pauses. "But not too much fun without me."

They are both insane. That is the only answer.

Rakiz escorts Nevada to the door, where his men are waiting. Zintas' bodies are strewn both inside and outside of the building, and Rakiz pulls Nevada close, taking her lips in a deep kiss. She raises her hand to his cheek, and I have to look away from their intimate moment.

I miss Ivy like a limb.

I turn back as Rakiz gestures to one of his men. Nevada quietly threatens all of the remaining warriors with pain and torture if they let her mate get hurt before finally allowing the male to lead her away.

The tribe king grins after her, his men fighting back their own smiles. It's clear that their queen is well loved.

Then we turn and stalk back inside. I will find out exactly where they have taken my little Flame Hair.

CHAPTER TWELVE

I^{vy}

Well, this is familiar.

I stare out at the crowd, and the crowd stares back. I'm standing next to a stage, waiting to be sold. Again.

Unlike on the slave planet, where we were sold out in the open, these guys are tense, eyeing the door of the large building warily. That doesn't stop them from leering at both me and the other unfortunate women who have ended up here though.

Also unlike on the slave planet, I'm not trembling in fear. Oh, I'm scared, for sure. But beneath anxiety lies a certainty that I haven't felt since before my dad died.

A certainty that there's someone in this universe that has my back.

Vrex will come for me. I know he will.

When it's my turn on the stage, I block out whatever bullshit is coming out of the alien's mouth as he lists my attributes. Instead, I run my eyes over the crowd, freezing when I see a Braxian standing to one side, close enough that I can see the flash of his white teeth as he grins at me. He winks one dark-green eye, and I realize he's not the only one here as I continue to survey the aliens in front of me.

Braxians are dotted throughout the crowd, and the Zintas haven't noticed them yet. Aroth stands in the front of the crowd with the group of Zintas he brought with him, and he smiles, flashing sharp teeth at me as my gaze lands on him.

Wow, buddy, these guys are gonna kick your ass.

I'm not paying any attention until a shove at my back tells me that I've been bought. An alien with dark-red skin stands next to the stage waiting for me, a leash in his hand, and I pause.

What if I'm wrong? What if Vrex isn't going to make it? My skin crawls as the red alien steps forward, his grin showcasing sharply pointed teeth.

That's when the room erupts into chaos.

A Braxian leaps forward and punches the red alien in the face. The alien drops like a stone while I gape at the Braxian, who hauls me into his arms.

"I can walk!"

"Quiet."

I growl. "Put me down, asshole."

"I was tasked with keeping you safe, female. And the Assassin of Agron is scarier than you are."

Awesome.

Swords are clashing, and I shudder as a piercing scream sounds. A group of Braxians are fighting in front of us, preventing anyone from getting close as they drive through the crowd and toward the door.

I look over my shoulder, where more Braxians are guarding our backs, cutting down anyone who gets close.

"Ivy!"

I crane my head toward the door. "Vrex?"

Someone has given him a sword, and he's fighting toward me like a berserker. The room is pandemonium, and I watch as Vrex reaches for a Zinta attempting to escape with one of the women, kicking him in the gut as he tries to flee. He picks up the blue-skinned woman and *throws* her to another Braxian, who plucks her out of the air, ignoring her screams.

There's a method to the madness, I realize. The Braxians have slaughtered most of the Zintas, along with anyone else dumb enough to attack or attempt to take one of the kidnapped woman with them.

He came for me. Like he promised he would.

God, I'm so fucking glad to see him alive.

He seems invincible as he fights his way toward me. Like a superhero. But he's still just a man.

I itch to join the fight. I push my hands against the Braxian's chest so I can get enough leverage to see over the crowd. He helpfully holds me a little higher, although he's not feeling cooperative enough to put me back on my feet.

I come perilously close to whining. "I want to fight!"

He ignores me, and I'm forced to watch as the Zintas attack. Aroth meets my gaze, his teeth bared as he drives toward me.

I raise my middle finger. Now, if only I could be the one to—

Vrex is suddenly there, and there's nothing but surprise on Aroth's face as he's impaled on my huge warrior's sword.

When did you start thinking of him as yours, Ivy?

The Braxian with the green eyes says something to Vrex,

whose mouth twitches as if he's thinking about smiling. Together, they cut down the remaining Zintas, while the rest of the Braxians take care of anyone who thought they could get away with buying and selling women.

Vrex is drenched with blood when he reaches me, but I don't care as he pulls me to him.

"Thank you," he says to the Braxian, who nods as he hands me over. The Braxian gives me a look like he's glad he doesn't have to deal with me anymore, and I send him a winning smile.

"If I'm not allowed to smile at other females, you can't smile at any other male," Vrex growls at me, but his eyes are lit with humor and relief as he cups my face.

"I'll try my best," I say, absurdly pleased to feel his arms around me.

Vrex lets me stand, and I stare around us at the carnage.

"Don't look at that," he says, his voice soft, and I lean up and kiss him. I've seen death and horror, but something about the way he wants to protect me from it melts my heart.

The warrior with the green eyes approaches.

"It is nice to see you alive," he says. "We have had warriors searching for you for days."

"This is Dexar," Vrex tells me, wrapping his arm around my waist and pulling me close. "He is the qatai of his tribe."

I examine the huge warrior. "It's nice to meet you."

He nods. "You too." He returns his attention to Vrex. "We need to leave before news of this spreads throughout this land."

The wave of his hand encompasses the room, and I carefully keep my eyes on his face, choosing to ignore the splashes of red in my peripheral vision.

"The females have been given credits and set free," one of the warriors announces, and Dexar nods.

"Good."

The low murmurs in the room drop to silence as Rakiz appears in the doorway, his face tight.

"Let's go," he says, and we all follow him out.

The people who live here are no longer minding their own business as they go about their day. Every single one of them stares at us, most of them in fear. There must be twenty Braxians with us, and we're traveling in a pack. Vrex has ensured that I'm safely in the middle of the group, surrounded by warriors, but my neck itches as we march through the silent streets.

It feels like an hour later when we finally reach the dock.

The first person I recognize is Nevada. She grins at me, striding forward to give me a hug.

"About damn time you showed up."

I laugh. "It wasn't my fault, I swear."

"Well, the others will be happy to know you've finally been found. Now we just need to find Charlie, and you guys can focus on getting home."

Vrex tenses at that, and I glance at him. Truthfully, I haven't even thought about getting back to Earth over the past few days.

More Braxians wait, some of them already seated on the Zintas' boat. I guess we're taking it with us. I'm fine with that.

Spoils of war.

Another boat sits next to it. A smaller boat—one small enough that I almost want to ask how the hell all those giant Braxian warriors managed to fit on it.

This boat may not be as large as the Zintas', but it's sleeker. It's a completely different design—the hull curved like the boats I've seen on Earth and a large sail waiting to be hoisted.

"Wow," I say. A scruffy older warrior is ordering around a few of the other Braxians, and they begin turning the boat, preparing to leave.

"I thought Braxians didn't travel across the water," I say.

The warrior turns. "We don't," he says. "This is the first time. It took me many revolutions to perfect my design and even longer to build this creation. Thankfully, these warriors arrived to help me finish it."

I blink at Vrex. "You *built* a boat to come find me?"

"Finished it," he says with a grin. "This is Yalex. He was kind enough to allow us to test out his contraption today."

The look that Yalex gives Vrex makes it clear that the older warrior didn't exactly have much choice in the matter. I open my mouth, but then I'm slamming it shut as Vrex suddenly turns, thrusting me behind him. He draws his sword as the other warriors do the same.

I turn to see what all the fuss is about, and my mouth drops open.

A Braxian stands in front of us. But he's like no Braxian I've seen before. His hair is shorter, and a gleaming black crown is angled jauntily on his head. His eyes are a deep midnight blue, and they scan me coolly before focusing on the warriors.

He's surrounded by guards, and I swallow as I compare their numbers to ours. This could be very, very bad.

"I heard rumors that there were invaders in our territory. One of my subjects came to me swearing that my streets were running red with blood," the Braxian says silkily.

Dexar, to his credit, doesn't look at all shaken by this new development. "The Zintas took one of ours. Perhaps you should warn your people against such a thing in the future. Especially now that we can cross the Colossal Water."

Wait. *His* people? This Braxian rules over all the creatures in this place?

"Well, consider me shook," I murmur to Vrex, and he slides me a look.

The king—because that's what he must be—smiles. It's not a very nice smile, and I shiver, stepping closer to Vrex.

"I had wondered about our cousins across the water, living in camps like primitives."

Rakiz bares his teeth in his own smile. "We had also wondered about the savages over here, allowing their subjects to cross the Colossal Water and trade in flesh."

I shiver at the look in the king's eyes. All the Braxians are threatening, especially the tribe kings, but this guy...

This guy is on a whole different level.

Nevada peers around Rakiz's shoulder. "Nice crown," she says. "Looks like—"

Rakiz slaps his hand over Nevada's mouth, and I choke on a laugh. She just can't help herself.

The king stares at her and then shifts his eyes back to me. All of the warriors bristle.

"Interesting creatures that you have chosen to mate with," he says.

"Creatures?" Now I'm the one who's offended. "Listen, you—" Vrex reaches for my hand, squeezing warningly, and I clamp my mouth shut. The king's midnight eyes scan us, missing nothing.

"I suggest that next time you come here, you refrain from killing my subjects."

From the way his guards are shifting on their feet, as if itching to fight, I'm guessing this is less of a suggestion and more of a threat.

Dexar doesn't look scared. But it's Vrex who steps forward.

"I suggest that next time you allow your subjects to kidnap our females, you prepare for war," he growls.

The king scans us again. Then, with one last nod, he turns and walks away, his guards trailing after him.

"Who the fuck was that?" Nevada demands, elbowing Rakiz in the ribs. She gives him a look that quite clearly says they'll be talking about the hand-on-mouth situation later.

He grins at her, but the grin quickly falls from his face as he glances at Dexar. "There have long been rumors about Braxians across the water. We may have assumed they would eventually be our allies, but this is obviously not the case."

He turns to the boats, and Yalex gives him a nod.

"Time to go," Rakiz says.

Vrex

Ivy is quiet as we travel across the Colossal Water. On the way across to where she was being held, all I could think of was her, my attention focused on whether she was safe.

Now that I have her wrapped in my arms, I refuse to lose her. Which is why I'm continually running my eyes over the water, scanning for threats.

"I could teach you to swim if you like," Ivy says softly. "Maybe not in this water though. God only knows what kinds of creatures would show up to nibble on us." She shudders, and I almost smile. There are not many things that seem to disconcert my little Flame Hair, but when it comes to the Colossal Water, we are in agreement.

"I would like to learn," I tell her. I will never forget the frustration and devastation I felt watching her be taken across the water.

"Thank you for coming for me." Her voice is small, and I lean down, brushing a kiss on her nose. I will always come for her. But after listening to Nevada talk with her about returning to her planet, I realized that Ivy may not want this.

Why *would* a brave, beautiful female like her want to stay with a male who makes others tremble with fear? A male who lives alone, far from the other human females on this planet—far even from other Braxians.

I glance behind us as Nevada moves down the boat toward us, Rakiz shadowing her footsteps. I'm reassured by the way he gazes at the water warily, pulling his mate close as she moves across the logs that somehow float on the Colossal Water.

Across from us, Dexar lounges on the other boat. When he notices us watching, he leans over, languidly trailing his hand in the water and raising one eyebrow as if in a dare.

I'm immediately bombarded by memories of the two of us as young children, when my mother was still alive. We battled to outdo each other, constantly attempting to win our continual war of one-upmanship.

Before we stepped onto these boats, Dexar leaned close.

"Now that you have ceased hiding in the woods like a child beneath his furs, perhaps we can talk about why you left my tribe," he murmured silkily before stalking away.

I pull my attention back to the present as Rakiz notices Dexar's taunting and sends him a lewd gesture, making Nevada laugh.

She sits down next to Ivy. "I saw your clues, by the way."

Ivy goes still. "Really?"

Nevada snorts. "Bright-pink material? Those pajamas

were hard to miss. I snuck away from Rakiz and went looking for you. Once he caught up with me—and after he finished beating his chest—he helped me search. We found Zoey, but you'd already been moved by that point."

"Is she...okay?"

"She's alive. The healers say she's getting stronger every day. If you hadn't left us those clues, we never would've found her."

Ivy leans her head back against my chest, her shoulders slumping. "And Beth?"

"She's doing well too. She's at Dexar's tribe with Alexis. When she escaped, she got caught in a Voildi's trap. It messed up her leg."

"Oh God. Beth was a dancer. A good one, from the few comments she made."

"Yeah. She's doing good though. The warrior who found her, he dotes on her. He reminds me of your guy," Nevada says, flicking me a glance. "The silent type."

Ivy tenses, opening her mouth. Is she about to refute that I'm her "guy"? She strokes my arm, and I realize I've tightened my hold on her. Nevada tilts her head, grinning at me.

"Let's see," Nevada says. "That just leaves Ellie, Vivian, and Charlie. Ellie's mated to Terex and completely knocked up." She laughs at whatever she sees on Ivy's face. "And Vivian's still praying that the Arcav will land here any day and take her back to the land of makeup and hairdressers."

"And Charlie?"

"That's what I was going to talk to you about." Nevada glances at me again. "How do you feel about going up against a dragon, big guy?"

Ivy

I'm still attempting to process everything Nevada has told me as we finally get close to land. Apparently, Charlie was taken by an actual fire-breathing dragon. The day before Ilax died, I asked Vrex about the gorgeous mermaid-like scales across his chest. He'd shrugged, simply saying that he was descended from the Great One.

Turns out, the Great One is a dragon, and he took Charlie. Apparently, the other women had kind of assumed that Charlie had been the dragon's lunch, since she was bleeding so heavily when she was taken. But Alexis saw her not long ago and said she looked fine, only she was obviously being held against her will by a huge, very angry dragon.

Did I mention that the dragon apparently breathes fire?

Vrex seemed unconcerned by this, simply nodding along as Nevada described how the dragon had stretched its huge wings, eyeing Alexis and Dexar like they'd taste great with barbecue sauce.

I fall asleep against Vrex. When I wake up, I have to blink a few times before I realize I'm not dreaming.

I'm on a mishua, still held in Vrex's arms. It's dark, and in the distance, I see lanterns burning ahead of us.

"This is Rakiz's camp." Vrex's voice is tight, and my chest aches at the reminder of how bad his life was when he lived in a camp just like this.

"Why are we here?"

"It's much closer than my tashiv. You need to rest. And you can see your friends."

My stomach twists. Does he not *want* me to go home with him?

Be cool, Ivy. You guys haven't talked about any of this stuff yet.

I nod. My head's spinning. I must've been in a deep sleep 'cause I'm insanely groggy. I glance to my right, where Rakiz has Nevada curled into his arms like a baby, her head buried in his neck as she sleeps.

Aw.

Vrex helps me off the mishua, and I give Nari's nose a stroke. A short, curvy woman steps forward, a huge smile on her face.

"You helped me make a sling out of my pajamas when we were following the Voildi," she murmurs.

I can't help but grin back at her. "I did. How are you, Ellie?"

A huge warrior joins her, wrapping an arm around her waist.

"I'm great. I'm glad you're okay. This is Terex, by the way."

The warrior nods at me, but it's clear that he only has eyes for Ellie. I drop my eyes to her stomach, and she laughs as she sees the direction of my gaze.

"Yup, it didn't take long before Nevada and I ended up barefoot and pregnant," she jokes, but it's clear that she's deliriously happy.

I attempt to ignore the stab of envy that slides through my gut like a knife. Vrex finishes handing Nari over to one of Rakiz's warriors, and Nevada snorts as she walks past, rubbing at her eyes.

"Speak for yourself," she says, dropping her gaze to Ellie's feet, which are, indeed, bare.

Terex frowns at this. "You should be wearing shoes, tiny female."

She smiles up at him. "I was excited to see these guys. It's okay, I'll go back to bed as soon as Ivy and Vrex are settled."

Vrex goes still next to me, and I have a feeling it's

because Ellie called him by his name and not the Goddamned Assassin of Agron.

Nevada calls over her shoulder to Ellie, "There's an empty kradi for these guys near yours."

Ellie nods, turning back to me. "We can figure out everything else tomorrow, but I'm sure you're tired right now."

"Exhausted," I say.

Vrex is quiet beside me as we trail after Ellie and Terex. They lead us to a large tent-like structure, and I almost kiss Ellie's bare feet when I poke my head into the attached bathing room. A woman is filling a large tub with water.

"I thought you guys would want to take a bath," Ellie says, chewing on her lip as she glances between Vrex and me. I'm suddenly awkward, but Vrex nods, and she smiles. We say our good nights, and the woman who was filling the bath grins at us as she leaves.

"God," I say, glancing between the pile of furs and the huge tub. "I'm so tempted to go back to sleep, but I need a bath so bad."

Vrex steps forward, and just like that, any awkwardness melts away as he takes my mouth with his.

"I will bathe you, little Flame Hair," he murmurs against my lips, and I blink at him. How am I suddenly this aroused when a moment ago, all I wanted to do was crawl between those furs and sleep for a week?

"That sounds amazing," I say, "but only if you'll get in there with me."

Vrex's sudden grin tells me exactly what he thinks of that idea, and I laugh.

We both strip, and I sigh as I hop into the warm water. Vrex slides in behind me, and a very different sound leaves my throat as I feel the long, hard length of him against me.

I lean against his chest, tilting my head up and back as

he leans down, brushing his mouth over mine. Once. Twice. On the third time, I groan.

"Tease."

He laughs against my lips, the sound low. I can feel him shaking behind me, and the thought of this huge warrior trembling as he tries to restrain himself...

I pull back, examining his face. I raise my eyes, meeting his burning gaze, and I shiver. I have...things to say to him. He runs his hand down, along my arm, his touch possessive, and all thought leaves my mind as he cups my breast, stroking my nipple.

He mutters a curse as it hardens for him, and I press kisses against his shoulders, throat, anywhere I can reach. I twist in the water, and Vrex cups my butt, holding me up before I can accidentally knee him in the nuts.

He smiles, that crooked smile he only gives me, and my eyes sting. "Thank you for coming for me," I murmur.

"Always," he vows.

He slants his mouth over mine, sliding his hand down to where I'm aching for him.

His mouth drops to my collarbone, and he kisses his way up my neck, paying special attention to the spot right beneath my ear. I break out in goose bumps, shivering in pleasure, and Vrex gently runs the edge of his teeth along the side of my throat.

His fingers are playing with me below the water, and I drop my head, pressing my forehead against his as I gasp.

I reach for him, and he growls as I take his hard cock in my hand, stroking up and down the length of him. Pleasure almost blinds me as he flicks my clit before thrusting two fingers into me.

"I need you," I say, and he doesn't argue, removing his fingers and positioning me on top of him.

I rock my hips, sliding down as I kiss the man who gives me more pleasure than I've ever known. He moves his fingers back to my clit, and I buck, my nails digging into his shoulders. How can I be this close already?

Vrex shifts both of his hands to my butt, the strength of him incredible as he raises me and lowers me back down as he thrusts up into me.

"Come for me," he murmurs against my lips, and I do, just as he angles me, hitting my G-spot.

I cry out his name as I tip my head back, my body melting in his arms. With a low groan, Vrex takes my hair in his hand, tilting my head so he can take my mouth as he empties himself inside me.

CHAPTER THIRTEEN

I vy

"Yoo-hoo," a voice says, and I lift my head. Truthfully, I should've gotten up before now, but I'm so comfortable lying here wrapped in Vrex's arms.

I glance at the kradi entrance, then pull the furs possessively over Vrex's body. "You can come in, Nevada."

She doesn't hesitate, waltzing in like she owns the place, which I guess she kind of does.

She nods to Vrex, who nods back, and then her gaze finds mine.

"I've been waiting for you guys to get up, but then I figured I may as well just come to you. I haven't had a chance to see the ship we landed here in yet. Rakiz took me to the other one—" She waves her hand as I raise an eyebrow. "I'll tell you all about that one later. But the piece of space junk we crash-landed in is probably the best shot at getting off this planet...for anyone who wants to leave, of course."

Vrex tenses next to me, and Nevada's face is blank, but I can see humor dancing in her eyes.

"And just how do you propose we fix an alien spaceship?" I ask.

"You remember Alexis? Long blonde hair, killer figure? She's mated to Dexar, so she's not going anywhere. But guess what she did on Earth?"

I shrug, wishing I could roll over and snuggle some more with Vrex, who's currently driving me crazy running his fingers over my upper thigh under the blanket.

"She was an astronautical engineer. She basically built spaceships." Nevada's voice is triumphant, and Vrex moves his hand away as we both stare at her. "Can you believe that shit?"

I clear my throat. "No."

Nevada narrows her eyes at me, obviously unimpressed that I'm not more excited. "Look, Rakiz has some boring meeting, and he said I can go check out this ship as long as Vrex goes with us." She glances at him, raising her eyebrow. "What do you say, big guy?"

He gives one sharp nod, and she grins.

"Excellent."

Both Vrex and I are silent as she leaves. In the back of my mind, I always imagined that I'd be able to get off this planet somehow. It was my goal from the moment we crashed. But once I spent more time with Vrex, I stopped daydreaming about arriving back on Earth. Somehow, I pushed the idea right out of my head.

Vrex rolls away, reaching for his pants. The silence is awkward. Truthfully, I don't *want* to leave him. But all I've brought to his life are pain and heartache. Does he want to return to his cabin in the woods where he can be alone?

I open my mouth to ask him, but a bell rings, and I reach for one of the furs, wrapping it around me.

"Yes?"

It's Ellie. "I thought I'd bring you guys some breakfast." She smiles at me as she places the tray on a small table. "I'm so glad you're safe. Nevada said you're going to go check out the ship?"

I nod. "Do you want to come with us?"

"I'm fine right here." She shakes her head, and I ignore the envy that blooms inside me at her sweet smile. She obviously has the complete certainty that comes with finding her place in the universe.

"I need to speak with Rakiz," Vrex says quietly. He stepped into the small bathing room while we were talking, I realize, and he's pulled on his clothes.

"Okay," I say, leaning up for a kiss. He brushes his lips against mine, and then he's gone.

I stare after him for a moment before returning my attention to Ellie. "You want to have breakfast with me?"

"Sure."

We sit at the small table, and Ellie fills me in about everything that's happened while I was away. Apparently, Zoey is almost recovered, and I can go see her before I leave with Nevada. Beth is at Rakiz's tribe, but Ellie's hoping for all of us human women to get together soon.

"What made you decide to stay here?" I blurt out, and she's quiet for a long moment.

"It was...Terex. He was like no one I'd ever met on Earth. I'm sure you know what I mean." She smiles. "You know, I never believed in soul mates until I met him. I thought maybe one day I'd settle down with my friend Tim. We liked each other just fine. We might've gotten married, maybe had children together. And I never would've known what this kind of love feels like. The 'do anything for him' kind of love."

My eyes sting, and Ellie's face falls.

"Did I say something?"

"It's nothing. I'm just tired. Probably an adrenaline crash from the last two days."

Ellie's eyes are shrewd. "You know, your warrior seems nice," she says, and I laugh.

"Vrex is many things, but I don't know if I'd ever describe him as 'nice.' We had a...moment, in that hole together. He promised that he'd always come for me. And he gave me this."

I hold up the gold pendant, and Ellie's eyes widen.

"It's beautiful."

"Yeah. I guess what I'm asking is...how did you know you wanted to give up your life on Earth...for a guy?"

She shakes her head. "It wasn't just for a guy," she says as she pops a piece of fruit in her mouth. "When I settled into life here, I just knew it was where I was always supposed to be. It felt like home. Terex was a large part of it, don't get me wrong. But I'd already decided I was going to stay before he declared his undying love for me." Her wide smile transforms her face from cute to beautiful.

"Why?"

"The people here are special. There's a real community in this camp. A family. I was happy to give up electricity for a chance to build a life here. With Terex."

I mull over this for a while as we eat in silence.

"I just don't know if Vrex is in it for the long haul, you know? We came pretty close to making promises to each other. The kind of promises you can't take back. But he's still a mercenary, and I'm still the woman he was paid to bring back."

"Well, for what it's worth, I hope you decide to stay."

I smile at her. "Will you take me to Zoey?"

She nods, and we're both quiet as we walk to the tent she calls the "healers' kradi."

It's large, with a bunch of beds placed several feet apart. For some reason, I expected the clinical, sterile smell of a hospital, but the kradi smells like herbs. Zoey is the only person using a bed, although a warrior is currently sitting in front of a woman who must be one of the healers while she bandages a wound in his arm.

Zoey's talking to a blonde woman who looks like she belongs on magazine covers, and the woman scans me from head to toe as I walk in.

I raise my eyebrow at her, and she grins right as Zoey notices me.

"Oh my God, they told me you were here, but I could barely believe it."

Tears roll down her face, and I leap forward, wrapping her in a hug.

"Good to see you alive," I tell her, and she chokes on a laugh.

"Likewise."

"You remember Vivian?"

Oh yes, I remember Vivian. I was tempted to deck her at one point when she wouldn't stop being a giant bitch to Ellie. From the smile on Ellie's face, there are no hard feelings, and she winks at me as she hands Zoey a cup of water.

Zoey leans against the pillows, catching her breath.

I eye her. "How are you feeling?"

She waves a hand. "I'm feeling like I'm sick of being on the receiving end of that exact look." She laughs.

Ellie narrows her eyes at her. "We're just worried. We're allowed to hover over you occasionally, considering you almost died."

Zoey rolls her eyes but gives Ellie an indulgent smile before raising her eyebrow at me. "You see what I have to put up with?"

I'm just glad she's alive to be annoyed at the smothering attention of both Vivian and two women who are practicing for motherhood. She grins at my expression, obviously reading my mind.

"Tell me everything," she says.

I fill her in, and she tells me all about how she got back here and her recovery process. Ellie jumps in occasionally, and we only stop chatting when one of the healers tells us that Zoey needs to rest.

"You know Tagiz will want a full report of what you did while he was away hunting," the healer murmurs, and Zoey rolls her eyes.

"He's so bossy."

Her eyes are sliding closed though, so I lean forward to say my goodbyes.

"I'm sorry I couldn't make it back for you," I murmur.

"Don't be ridiculous," she says with a yawn. "I knew you'd do everything you could. It was worth being alone for a while when I heard Killis screaming about you taking his eye."

Ellie looks a little green at that, and I laugh.

"He's dead, you know," Zoey mumbles. "Killis. The Voildi tried to attack one of the tribes."

I smile. "Sounds like the past few weeks have been eventful for everyone."

I turn my head as Vrex appears in the kradi, and my heart flutters at the heated look he gives me.

"Are you ready?" he asks.

I smile. "Yup."

***

Ivy

"What a piece of shit," Nevada says as we stare at the ship.

"Yeah," I say.

In the bright sunlight, it reminds me of a rusty tin can.

Vrex makes us wait while he checks out the ship, and then he returns, giving us a nod.

"I will wait here," he says, his gaze constantly scanning our surroundings. We're close to his house, I realize. Does he want to return to his peace and quiet?

I nod and leave him with the other warriors, who spread out to guard the area.

We climb the stairs, and Nevada wrinkles her nose. "Wow, it stinks in here."

It sure does. Nevada moves restlessly around the space, and I give her a moment alone when she moves downstairs to see the cage we were locked in together.

"Do you ever think of the other women?" she asks me suddenly as she reappears. "The ones who were sold to other people? And the ones who stayed on the ship?"

I nod. "Yeah, all the time. This planet has been so hard. But we got lucky compared to what some of those women are probably going through."

Nevada runs her gaze over the control center while I stare at the blinking light.

"Ivy?" Something in her voice tells me this isn't the first time she's said my name.

"We have a problem," I tell her. I count the seconds once

more just to be sure, and then I curse. "That light is flashing way faster than it was the last time we were here."

Nevada narrows her eyes on it, as focused as if she's hunting and the light is her prey. "What do you think it is?"

"I'd love to get Alexis to check it out," I say. "I could be wrong—I hope I am—but I think it's some kind of GPS signal. And the fact that it's blinking faster..."

Nevada's face goes white. "You think they're coming back."

"Yeah."

We're both silent for a long moment as we stare at the light. Nevada runs her hands over it, throwing me a questioning look at the giant cracks from where Vrex attempted to smash it.

"Why would they come back?" she murmurs.

"We're nothing but products to them," I choke out. "Products they bought and paid for. What if they want to find those products so they can sell them? Maybe they just want to see if their ship can still fly."

The color returns to Nevada's face as her eyes glitter in rage. She strokes the sword at her side. "If they try to take us off this planet..."

I don't say what we're both thinking. That any alien race advanced enough to travel through space will likely be armed with weapons that the warriors on this planet would have no hope of matching.

"We need to prepare in case you're right," Nevada says. "If they are coming back, we need to find better weapons. We need a fucking army."

I nod, and we both stare at the light for a few more moments. Then bile creeps up my throat, and Nevada lets out a string of curses that would make a sailor on Earth blush.

"It just got faster," she says.

"Yeah."

Vrex

Ivy's face is pale as death when she exits the ship and moves toward me. I reach for her, and she buries her head in my chest. She's shaking, I realize.

"What's wrong?"

She's silent, and I glance behind her to where Nevada is tense, her face cold.

"We think the aliens who bought us might be coming back," Nevada says.

Ivy pulls away, looking up at me silently. She's terrified.

"I made you a promise, little Flame Hair," I say.

She blinks up at me.

"No one will take you from me."

A tear falls from her eye, and I wipe it away. She smiles, her mouth quivering. "You always know what to say."

It seems she doesn't quite believe my words, but that is okay. I will do whatever I must to keep her safe. I glance at Nevada, who is getting ready to mount the mishua that's tied to mine. I know Rakiz feels the same. And Dexar would never allow anyone to take his qatal from him.

This morning, when Nevada mentioned using the ship to leave this planet, Ivy did not protest. Did not tell Nevada that she would stay with me. I gaze down at her beautiful face as I remember the vows I made to her in that hole across the Colossal Water. Does she not believe me? Or does she not want to stay with the Assassin of Agron?

We're all silent as we mount our mishua, and I can't help

but pull Ivy close as I sit behind her. Ivy has explained to me how this GPS works, and while it sounds like sorcery, I can understand her fear. If the blinking light is not this GPS she speaks of, then we do not need to worry.

But if it is...

We must prepare for the worst.

A dark shadow falls over us, and we all glance up.

"Holy shit," Nevada says. "Is that—"

"Charlie!" Ivy screams. There's no reply from the figure who is currently riding the dragon as if it is a mishua. The dragon turns toward its territory, and it's obvious that neither of them have noticed us as they get further and further away.

We're all silent. I turn and find one of Rakiz's guards staring at me.

"Was that—"

"The Great One," I breathe. "Yes."

Ivy is peering at the spot where the dragon just disappeared, while Nevada turns to us both.

"Are you guys thinking what I'm thinking?"

We both look at her, and she throws up her hands.

"We may not have fancy technological weapons, but Charlie was just riding a motherfucking dragon. *Riding* it. As if she was out for a Sunday horseback ride."

Ivy stares at her. "You think that dragon would help us?"

"I think if it's letting her ride him, maybe it'd also be willing to blow some flames at any purple assholes who decided to land on this planet."

She strokes a hand over the small bump of her stomach. "I'm not being taken from Rakiz. So if our best chance is a dragon? That's what we need to use."

CHAPTER FOURTEEN

I vy

All of us are silent on our way back to camp. When we arrive, Vrex helps me off the mishua but doesn't move to follow me into camp.

"What's wrong?" I ask, searching his face. His expression is hard, but his eyes...there's something in them that I don't quite recognize.

"Nothing. I have something that I must do," he tells me. "I will be back tomorrow."

"Tomorrow?" My mouth drops open, and Nevada moves away, giving us privacy as I attempt to deal with this bombshell.

He nods, and I try to tamp down the panic that's threatening to rise up and take over my mouth.

"Are you...leaving me?" He was happy in his cabin in the woods alone. Maybe he's realized that he was happier there than with me and all this drama.

"No." He takes my hand in his and pulls me close. "I will return. I promise."

My eyes burn, and I swallow around the lump in my throat. When did I get so needy? It's that thought that makes me pull my hand away with a smile.

"Okay," I manage. "Sounds good. I'll see you tomorrow."

I don't ask where he's going. He would have told me if he wanted me to know. Instead, I step back.

"Ivy—"

"Travel safe." I turn and walk back into camp, ignoring the sympathetic look that Nevada sends me.

The sun is setting, and I wander toward the kradi I shared with Vrex last night. I change direction at the thought of being alone, heading back toward the healers' kradi.

"Ivy?"

I whirl. "Beth?"

She jumps toward me, laughing and pulling me into a hug. I blink.

"Wow," I say, closing my eyes as she squeezes me tight. "It's so good to see you."

Beth pulls away, her eyes wet. "You too. I'm sorry I couldn't get back to you." She moves back a few feet, and I note the slight limp of her gait.

"I'm just glad you got to safety. I heard you were hurt."

She nods. "Yeah." Her expression is sad for a moment, but then her delicate face lights up like the sun. "This is Zarix," she says, and the huge warrior gives me a grin as he reaches us.

"Thank you for encouraging Beth to escape," he says.

Beth snorts. "Encouraging? I believe the last words she said to me were 'Buck up, champ. You're on.'"

I can't help but laugh. "Yeah, I'm all about that tough love."

Beth glances behind me. "Alexis, come see Ivy."

I didn't remember which woman was called Alexis when Nevada mentioned her, but I definitely remember her gorgeous face, long blonde hair, and light-blue eyes. She looks like she should be tanning on a beach somewhere.

"I remember you," Alexis says. "The firefighter."

"That's me. That feels like a lifetime ago though."

"Girl, I hear you."

"What are you guys doing here? Not that it's not great to see you..."

Alexis gestures toward the healers' kradi. "Ellie, Vivian, and Zoey are waiting for us. Zarix was planning to meet Dexar here for his meeting with Rakiz, so we figured we'd all join him and finally get to spend some time together."

"That sounds amazing." And a perfect way to distract myself from wondering where Vrex is going and what exactly it is that he's doing.

We make our way to the healers' kradi, where Nevada is also waiting for us. She raises her eyebrow at me as I enter, silently asking if I'm okay. I nod. Maybe I'll pick her brain about Vrex later. After all, she seems to have an enviable relationship with her warrior.

Is that what you want? A relationship? On Agron?

I stare at the walls of the kradi while the other women greet each other.

I...do. With Vrex. The warrior who just took off to God knows where without any warning.

I force myself to focus on the conversation around me. While everyone is laughing and catching up, the subject continually turns to Charlie.

"Well," Alexis says, "how are we going to get her back?"

Ellie chews on her lip. "From what Nevada just told me, it doesn't sound like she's being hurt, at least."

Beth tilts her head. "What do you mean?"

I describe the sight of the small figure perched on the dragon's back, her body tiny compared to the huge beast. Everyone is silent for a long moment.

Zoey coughs and blushes as we all glance at her. "Is it possible it could be a…friendly dragon?"

Alexis snorts. "It sure as hell wasn't friendly when Dexar and I saw them. I thought it was going to turn us to ash at one point."

Nevada frowns. "But you said it wasn't hurting Charlie, right?"

"Right."

I snort. "So all we know right now is that Charlie was taken by a dragon and now she's somehow using it as her form of transportation."

Vivian lets out a low whistle. "Why hasn't she flown it toward us, then?"

We all contemplate this for a moment.

"I remember Dexar calling the dragon 'possessive,'" Alexis murmurs. "Maybe it's nice to Charlie and only Charlie."

"Well," I say, "that's a problem. Because that dragon may be our only hope if those aliens come back."

Zoey turns sheet white. No one has told her, I realize. Nevada turns to the group as everyone begins talking at once, and I sit back while she explains our theory.

Alexis nods. "It could be some kind of GPS system. But it could be something else too. I'll get Dexar to take me to it tomorrow. Maybe I can try and disable it or something."

I blow out a breath in relief. "If not, we're going to need a backup plan. These warriors might be the scariest motherfuckers on this planet, but they're only armed with swords. So the only real backup plan we have is that dragon."

Zoey looks so pale that if she weren't lying down, I'd worry that she was going to pass out. I still remember the sound of her ribs cracking as one of those purple aliens kicked her on the slave planet. No wonder she's scared.

"Sure," Nevada says grimly. "But how do we get a giant, fire-breathing dragon to cooperate?"

None of us have any ideas.

***

Ivy

I wait all day for Vrex. Then I pace our kradi for most of the night as well.

He said he'd come back. Did he change his mind?

As soon as the sun rises the next morning, I head to Rakiz's tashiv. The guards have obviously been instructed to let me pass because they simply nod at me as I knock on the door.

Nevada opens it and gestures for me to come in. Alexis and Beth left yesterday, but we all promised to get together soon.

There was something incredible about being together with a group of women who've all been through the same experience. I've never had many girlfriends. Spending all your time working in a male-dominated industry will do that to you, and I was mostly a tomboy growing up. But I'm on my way to becoming fast friends with most of the other women.

I'm still on the fence about Vivian, and she grinned at me when I left the healers' kradi, as if reading my mind.

There was no malice in the grin, and I invited her to join me for lunch one day soon.

"That sounds great," she said.

As much as I've always felt like one of the guys, it was... nice to hang out with the other human women. To come together and try to figure out a plan to find Charlie and prepare, just in case the purple aliens come back.

We didn't come up with much, but whatever happens, we'll face it together.

Nevada points me toward a few comfortable-looking chairs near an unlit fire. "You hungry?"

"No." In fact, my stomach has been roiling with tension since it got dark yesterday and I accepted that Vrex wasn't returning.

Nevada's gaze examines me. "What's up?"

"I'm actually hoping to talk to your mate."

The word still feels weird to say, and Nevada winks at me as if she's reading my mind.

"Rakiz," she calls, and a door opens, revealing Rakiz with a fur slung low around his hips.

If I hadn't seen Vrex naked, I'd be taking a mental picture of the tribe king's eight-pack.

He raises his eyebrow. "Yes?"

"Vrex never returned yesterday."

I was hoping he wouldn't look worried. That he'd wave a hand and tell me that there was nothing to worry about. But his eyes sharpen, narrowing on my face.

"He left alone?"

I nod, and Rakiz frowns. "One of our hunting parties was attacked yesterday. Most of the Voildi are dead after they attempted to attack a Braxian tribe, but those who are still alive are desperate for food and supplies. The hunting party all survived, but..."

"But Vrex was traveling alone."

He angles his head. "Did he tell you where he was going?"

"No." The tribe king's gaze turns curious at that, and I feel my cheeks redden. Yes, the warrior I've been sleeping with every night just disappeared with no warning. And no, I have absolutely no idea where he could've gone, unless he ditched me to go hang out alone in his house in the woods.

My chest tightens. What if Vrex was attacked by an entire pack of Voildi? He's an incredible fighter, but he's still injured.

"Can you send some warriors after him?" I ask.

Rakiz gives me a sympathetic look. "We have groups of warriors already hunting, and I will send messengers asking them to warn Vrex if they see him. But with no way to know where he went..."

I nod, and Nevada reaches for my hand.

"Vrex is a huge, mean son of a bitch. I'm sure he's fine."

I nod again, but my stomach is twisting. I mumble my goodbyes, my mind elsewhere, and then I practically sleep-walk back to my kradi.

I'm sitting on the bottom step of the staircase when they arrive. Mom opens the door, and I hear a sound I've never heard her make before. The kind of sound our dog Jax made when he was hit by a car.

I peer around the bannister. There are two men at the door, and I recognize one of them. He works with my dad. His eyes meet mine, and they're so full of sympathy that I immediately know what has happened.

Mom falls to her knees, slapping at the men as they attempt to help her to her feet. She's howling now, her hands gripping her hair as she rocks back and forth.

Dad went into the towers. And he's never coming out.

I'm shaking, sick to my stomach as I pace. Is this what's about to happen to Vrex? Am I about to learn that he was attacked and he's never coming back?

I can't face the other women, and they seem to understand, giving me space. I spend a few hours near the camp entrance, and then I return to our kradi, where I pace until I fall into an exhausted heap on our furs.

Tears run down my face as I stare at the wall. I should've told him not to leave. Should've asked him to stay with me. Should've made it clear to him that I want to stay on Agron.

I hiccup as I pull my knees close, curling into a ball. I can't even imagine returning to Earth at this point. Can't imagine leaving Vrex behind.

But he left you.

He said he was just going to be away for one day. Something has happened to him. I know it has.

I wipe my face. Fuck this. If he's not back by sunrise, I'm going after him myself.

Vrex

I scowl down at the dead Voildi. The creatures blocked most of the roads back to camp, lying in wait for anyone stupid enough to not recognize one of their traps.

After what happened last time, I immediately turned around as soon as I spotted a fallen tree on the road through the forest. I decided that taking the long way back to camp—close to Dexar's tribe—would be the better choice.

Unfortunately, Nari was hauling a cart of supplies, and this made her slower than usual. We barely managed to escape that pack of Voildi only to be attacked by another pack when I approached camp from a different direction.

Dexar's warriors were in the area, and it is only due to their swift actions that I am alive.

A pack of more than twenty Voildi waited for me, obviously those who had fled the battle for Tecar's tribe. They took one look at the cart attached to my mishua and grinned at me, their lean faces demonstrating that they have found few options for food in this territory.

Braxian traps are well guarded, and if they had come across a group of our hunters, they would have been slaughtered.

Ivy's name was on repeat in my head throughout the fight.

I had to get back to her. Had to convince her to stay with me. The thought of her getting on that crumpled spaceship and leaving me on this planet alone...

My inattention cost me, and an enterprising Voildi slipped beneath my guard while I swung my sword at his friend.

The smell of my own blood filled my nose.

I blink, returning my attention to the present.

"We offer our healers' kradi on behalf of our qatai," one of the warriors says, and I tilt my head.

"Your name is Tazo, correct?"

He nods, and I sigh. I remember training with this male when we were young. He has no reason to kill me. In fact, my death at the hands of one of Dexar's warriors would cause the qatai shame and a loss of face, given that he still owes me one more favor.

My blood is warm, dripping through my hand as I hold it clamped to my side. Dexar's camp is several hours closer than Rakiz's.

But Ivy...

I picture her waiting for me, pacing the kradi the way she would pace in my tashiv.

What if she does not believe that I will return?

"I need to go back to Rakiz's camp."

Tazo lifts one eyebrow, turning his gaze to the steady drip of my blood. "If it is a female you are hoping to return to, perhaps you should ask yourself if she would be pleased with the return of your dead body."

I bare my teeth at him, frustration warring with useless rage. This trip was supposed to help me convince Ivy to stay with me. Now she will believe I have abandoned her.

But Tazo is correct. If I know one thing about my little Flame Hair, it is that she is a logical female. She would not want me to return only to die on the way.

If that were to happen, her rage would likely follow me all the way to the afterlife.

CHAPTER FIFTEEN

I vy

I pace the camp walls. After much pleading on my part and a long talk with Nevada, Rakiz has finally agreed to let me take five of his warriors and search for Vrex. Nevada seemed surprised that Rakiz had given in, but she whispered to me that he seems concerned about Vrex as well.

I have no real plan other than to head in the direction of Vrex's tashiv. If I arrive and he's gone back to living his hermit life, I'll kick his ass. Then I'll come back here to live out my days as the camp tramp.

Vrex isn't the only good-looking warrior around here.

I snort. Who am I kidding? Unfortunately, he's the only man for me. And when I find him, I'm going to give him a piece of my mind for making me worry this much.

My whole life, I've been afraid of letting people get too close. If I'm honest, my fear was a big part of the problem between Steve and me. Sure, my schedule was crazy, but I never opened up enough to truly let him in.

In the back of my mind, I was always terrified that I'd be that woman pacing back and forth near the front door, waiting to hear if her husband was alive. God knows it's easier to be the one risking death yourself than to be the one waiting at home.

And now look at me.

All those walls I put up were for nothing. Vrex has knocked them all down, and if he's dead...

I don't know if I'll survive it.

"Are you ready?"

I stop in my tracks, turning to Hewex, one of the warriors Rakiz is sending with me. He's already saddled up the mishua, and he gestures for me to come closer to mount the mishua he's tied to his own.

The other warriors are waiting behind him, and I attempt a smile as they nod at me.

I move closer, and that's when Hewex glances behind me, a grin spreading over his craggy face.

"Where do you think you're going?

I whirl, a sob leaving me at Vrex's gruff voice. He looks exhausted, sliding off his mishua as I run toward him. He pulls me into his arms, and I tremble against him as relief hits me like a drug.

"Where the hell were you?" I demand.

I pull back, thumping him in the chest, and he catches my hand, bringing it to his mouth. He kisses my palm and then gestures behind him.

His mishua is pulling a cart. Behind her, a group of Braxian warriors sit, watching us in amusement.

"Vrex," a voice says, and I turn as Rakiz and Nevada arrive. Nevada shoots me a relieved look, and I nod as Rakiz steps forward to slap Vrex on the back. "What happened?" he asks.

Vrex's mouth twists. "I was attacked on my way back. There were too many of the Voildi. Luckily, Tazo happened to be in the area. My wound was severe enough that it made more sense to travel to Dexar's tribe, which was closer. I came as soon as the healer allowed me to."

I feel the blood drain from my face, and Vrex gazes down at me, his eyes concerned.

"I was going to send a messenger," he says. "But I would have beaten them here."

"It's true," one of the warriors says. "He rode as if he was being chased by Dragix himself."

One of the other warriors snorts, and I nod.

"Where did you go?" I ask Vrex.

He tenses and glances around us. "That's something that I must talk to you about," he says.

Just because he wants to talk doesn't mean he's breaking up with you, Ivy.

"Okay." I glance around. "I'll meet you in our kradi?"

He nods, and I take off, grateful for a few moments to collect myself. Something about the way he's acting makes me think that he's nervous.

I don't pace any longer. I simply sit on the furs and contemplate the roof of the kradi. Vrex doesn't keep me waiting for long.

"I have something important to talk to you about," he says. "But I am not ready. There is...something that I need to have done first."

I scowl at him. "You know, this mysterious bullshit is starting to piss me off."

"Your friend has been sighted."

My mind is blank for a moment, and then it clicks. "Charlie?"

He nods. "If you want to attempt to speak to her, now is the time. But we have to leave immediately. I promise, we will speak about...us when we return."

I eye him. He's nervous again. As much as I want to push him, his words make sense. Finding Charlie is important for all of us.

"Fine."

He looks at me for a long moment, and then he strides forward, taking my hand to pull me to my feet.

"I know I am...difficult," he says. "I know I don't deserve your patience. But I'm asking for it anyway."

I sigh and lean my head against his chest. His scent envelops me—leather and sunshine.

"You should've taken your necklace back," I say, raising my head as he stiffens. "You're the one who needed the protection, not me."

He smiles gently down at me. "We will talk about this soon. For now, let's see if we can find your friend."

The mishua are still saddled, and it must take less than ten minutes for us to leave the camp.

Once we get close to the area where the dragon was spotted, we split into pairs. Rakiz and Nevada head west, two other pairs of warriors search in the south and east, while Vrex and I go north, toward the river.

After what must be an hour of fruitless searching, we're almost ready to give up.

"She must have left already," I say, depressed.

Vrex pulls me close and kisses my forehead as we gaze down the hill to the river. The water isn't rushing as fast here, and I'm tempted to take off my shoes and paddle my feet.

"Ivy," Vrex says, amusement in his low voice. "Look."

I follow his gaze further down the river, to the opposite side, and my mouth drops open.

Charlie is butt naked, splashing in the river like she doesn't have a care in the world.

Until she sees us, that is.

She lets out a sound that can only be described as a shriek, crouching down and hiding behind a large boulder.

Vrex tenses next to me, taking my hand, and I follow his gaze to the bank of the river. The dragon is lying in the sun, his eyelids at half-mast as he stares at us. As I watch, he flicks his tail before opening his mouth in a yawn, flashing rows upon rows of sharp white teeth.

I return my attention to Charlie, who is still hiding in the water. The dragon gazes at her, and something about the way he tilts his head makes me think he's...amused.

I walk down the hill and close to the river, Alexis's warning ringing in my ears. The dragon may look like an alligator basking in the sun, but something about the lazy flick of that huge tail is all the warning I need.

"Charlie?"

She peers at me from over the rock and then glances at the dragon. "You could hand me my towel, you know."

I blink, but she's still staring at the dragon, who glances at her and seems to sigh as he gets to his feet. I wish he wouldn't because the sight of his huge form moving that quickly...

It's more than a little terrifying. Especially when he uses one claw to swipe a long piece of material from where it's lying over a rock before throwing it to Charlie, who catches it out of the air as if they've done this a hundred times before.

I pinch myself. Nope, definitely not dreaming.

Charlie wraps the towel around herself and stands, moving out of the river and onto the bank. She walks through the water, slightly closer to us, sending the dragon a look when he flashes his teeth.

I have no words.

"Um. Hi," I say.

She grins at Vrex and me. "Hi. Excuse the grumpy dragon. He hasn't had enough to eat today."

Vrex tenses further beside me, obviously taking the words as a threat.

Charlie sighs. "He's not going to hurt you. We've come to an understanding."

I blink at her. An understanding with a huge, deadly dragon. Right.

"Uh, okay, then. We've been looking for you for a while now."

Color creeps up her cheeks. "Yeah, I'm sorry. It took a while before Dragix and I reached that understanding."

I frown at that. How exactly does she talk to the dragon? Do they communicate through growls and snarls? I glance at Vrex, but he's still focused on the dragon. *Dragix*, I remember with a glance back at Charlie.

Charlie seems to see where my mind is going because she smiles. "We've been in negotiations. I want to come hang out with you guys, but Dragix isn't the biggest fan of the Braxians."

Okay, so she obviously *can* communicate with the dragon in some way.

"That's why I'm here," I say. "We need your help."

Charlie tilts her head, looking entirely comfortable standing on the bank of the river with only a towel wrapped around her. She listens as I explain our theory about the purple aliens returning, and the dragon moves closer to her as she shivers.

"You really think they're coming back?" she asks.

"I think we should hope for the best but prepare for the worst."

The dragon looms over her before ducking its head and nuzzling up close. One gold eye focuses on me, and I glance away, unwilling to get into a staring contest with something that would consider me a snack. Vrex has obviously had enough because he steps forward, shielding my body with his.

The dragon snorts, and I stare as small plumes of smoke travel up from both his nostrils. Charlie reaches out, stroking a hand down his snout, and he seems to calm.

She's a fucking dragon whisperer.

"So what do you say?" I ask. "We're outgunned and likely to be outnumbered."

"I want to help." Charlie chews on her lower lip. The dragon stares at her, and her chin juts out as she narrows her eyes at him. "We need to discuss this," she says to me. "But you can count on *my* help, even if *Dragix* doesn't quite feel up to the task."

Ooh, a little reverse psychology for the dragon. I pinch myself again.

The dragon angles his head, staring at Charlie for a long moment before turning his attention to Vrex. Vrex is so still it seems as if he's not even breathing. When did he grab his sword? He's holding it loosely in his hand, and my chest tightens. How did I manage to find a guy who would fight a *dragon* for me?

Dragix seems to be tired of the conversation because he reaches out a huge clawed foot and pulls Charlie close. Charlie rolls her eyes at me as he nudges her onto his foot, and she sits down, still wrapped in the towel. She folds her legs under her as if she's sitting at a picnic, and I gulp as the dragon thrusts out his wings, casting a shadow over the riverbank on both sides of the water.

"We'll talk about this," Charlie calls. "Tell everyone I'll come see them as soon as I can."

And then they're gone.

***

Ivy

After we fill in the rest of the group on our little visit with Charlie and her pet dragon, we're all silent as we make our way back to the camp. I glance at Vrex occasionally, but he seems deep in thought, his brow furrowed as he gazes into the distance.

By the time we arrive, I've had about enough of my man of mystery.

"Listen," I say as he helps me dismount. "We need to talk, and we need to do it now."

He glances at me and then away, and I try to ignore the squeezing sensation in my chest. This does not bode well.

My heart is thundering as he nods, taking my hand.

"I have something to show you," he says. "I hope it is finished."

Now I'm really intrigued.

He hands over both of our mishua to the warriors responsible for looking after the beasts, and then I follow him into the camp. The sun is low in the sky, and silence stretches between us as I trail after my warrior.

He stops at a large kradi I've never seen before. It's close to the river and Ellie and Terex's kradi and not far from Rakiz and Nevada's tashiv.

I steel myself as he gestures for me to enter, and the breath leaves my lungs in shock as I glance around. "What... is this?"

Vrex shifts on his feet as I glance at him before returning my attention to the kradi. It's beautiful, and I wander through it before I can stop myself. In the main room, the wooden chairs from Vrex's tashiv are now sitting next to gorgeous brightly colored pillows, all surrounding a long table. In the bedroom, the intricately carved bedside tables I admired have been placed next to the same bed we first made love in.

Vrex is silent behind me as I poke my head into the bathroom.

"I couldn't bring the bath," he says. "I will get a new one."

I turn back to him, taking in his glittering eyes and tight jaw. "Okay, now you really need to tell me what's going on."

He takes my hand and pulls me to the bed before sitting beside me. Then he gets straight back to his feet as if he can't stay still.

"You're freaking me out," I say into the silence.

A breath shudders from him. "I know you want to go back to your home," he says. "I know I have nothing to offer you compared to your life on your planet. But I'm asking you to stay anyway."

I blink at him. "You're asking me to stay?"

One sharp nod.

"I thought you were breaking up with me."

His eyes widen, and he angles his head as he stares down at me. "Breaking up with you?"

"I thought you were showing me your bachelor pad." I

feel my cheeks heat at his incredulous expression, and he drops to his knees in front of me.

"I'm sorry I left. It was only supposed to be for a few hours. I brought these things here because I want you to be close to your human friends. I thought if I moved here, you might stay with me."

My mouth has dropped open. He gave up his favors for me. He's left his tashiv in the forest for me. Somehow, this incredible, loyal man thinks I'm worth it.

I'm not going to be the one to tell him differently.

His face falls slightly at my silence. "If you don't wish to stay on this planet, will you at least stay with me until you leave?"

"Vrex—"

"I thought I wanted to be alone. Thought I would *always* be alone. And then you stepped into my life. I was asleep, and you woke me up. I was barely breathing, and you gave me air. I know I'm not like other males. I know I'm...different. But I can try to be better."

My eyes sting, and I get to my feet. "You know, I went my whole life convinced it was a mistake to let people get too close. But you slipped beneath my defenses without even trying. I love you, Vrex. I think I loved you the moment I realized you'd made those shoes for me. I don't want you to be different. Ever."

His eyes widen in disbelief, but he reaches out, pulling me close. His hands cup my face, and then tears are slipping down my cheeks at the tenderness in his eyes.

"Will you...be my mate?"

My breath catches. I've seen the gorgeous gold rope wrapped around some of the other women's wrists, of course. But I never imagined that I'd meet a guy who wanted to be with me so much that he'd tie himself to me for the rest of his life.

"Of course."

He gently brushes my tears away, leaning down to take my mouth.

"I'm still mad at you for making me worry about you," I mumble against his lips, and he reaches up, stroking his hand down my hair.

"I know," he says. "I'm sorry." Then he kisses me again, and all I care about is that he's here, with me. If I have it my way, that's how we'll always stay.

His lips are warm, coaxing, and I relax further, my muscles turning languid as I lean against him. And then I yelp as he lifts me into his arms before laying me back on the furs.

He follows me down, pressing kisses along my neck, and a shudder ripples through me in response. This man makes me feel things I never expected to feel. I sink my fingers into his hair, angling my face until I find his lips again. His breath catches, and I smile against his mouth.

"You enjoy making me lose control," he says as he pulls away, his eyes the whiskey color I love so much.

"You make me lose control. Why shouldn't I do the same to you?"

He laughs, and I feel my smile widen at the sound. Then he's pulling off my clothes, and I'm helping him. I reach for his shirt, and he shrugs out of it before catching my hand in his and pressing a kiss to my palm.

My eyes sting at the tenderness on his face, and then he kisses me again, this time harder, deeper, pressing me back into the soft furs.

My head is spinning, and I groan out a protest as he moves away, but then he's kissing my breasts, and I bury my hands in his hair again, holding him close as he makes me lose my mind.

His calloused palm moves across my stomach, and then he takes my nipple into his mouth, rolling and playing as his hand moves lower, down to the warm heat of me.

He strokes his fingers over my clit, the movement light, teasing, designed to drive me out of my mind. My entire body tenses, and I'm shaking against him as his mouth moves to my other breast, and those fingers tease me, moving to a new spot each time I get close to losing my mind.

"Are you trying to drive me crazy?" I groan, and his low laugh makes my thighs clench around his hand.

Suddenly, he's inside me, thick and hard, and he catches my gasp in his mouth as he starts thrusting in earnest. I cry out, and he growls against me as I wind my legs around his hips so he can get even deeper.

He speeds up, and I urge him on, clutching at his shoulders as he slips one hand down, stroking my clit in time with his thrusts.

"I love you," he murmurs, and I clench around him, so close to ecstasy I can almost taste it.

"I love you too," I whisper, and my chest aches as he leans in to claim my mouth.

He changes the angle of his thrusts, plunging deep, and I suck in a breath.

Then I'm exploding, trembling as I arch in pleasure, and Vrex buries his face against my neck as he shudders in release.

EPILOGUE

I vy

Alexis pokes her head into the tashiv, a grin on her face. She looks gorgeous as usual, but her eyes widen as she stares at me.

"Wow," she says. "You're a total fox."

I laugh. Today's the day of my mating ceremony, and I couldn't be happier.

Alexis and Beth are waiting for their own mating ceremonies until Charlie has been found. I thought about doing the same, but when I kept waking up to find Vrex staring at me, his brow furrowed as if he couldn't believe I was still lying next to him, I changed my mind.

Vrex has been hurt time and time again over the years. He's been treated like nothing more than the Assassin of Agron, and everywhere he goes, people whisper and cower in fear. I want to prove to him that I'm committed to him for the rest of our lives.

That's why I convinced the other women to help me with a surprise mating ceremony.

"I can't believe I thought this was a good idea," I murmur. Butterflies have taken over in my stomach, and I'm glad I haven't eaten yet this morning because I feel like I could throw up.

Ellie smiles at me. "This *is* a good idea. You know your warrior better than anyone else, and I'm sure you're right when you say he wouldn't want a big, public ceremony."

Of that I'm sure. "But what if he wanted to help plan the ceremony?"

Nevada catches my eye, and we stare at each other for a moment before we both burst out laughing. Okay, so the chance that Vrex wants to have any input when it comes to our mating ceremony is low.

I'm still nervous though.

"You look beautiful," Vivian says, and I smile at her. She's helped me plan every aspect of this ceremony and even found me a gorgeous dress to wear. It's a deep-crimson red that I never would've selected on my own. But once she bullied me into putting it on, I had to admit that the color actually works.

"I'd kill for your hair," Ellie says. "Vrex is going to lose his mind when he sees you."

"If I don't barf down my dress first."

Nevada smirks at me. "Buck up, champ," she says. "You're on."

I groan, but I can't help but laugh. "And so we've come full circle."

Zoey steps up next to Alexis. "Beth has gone to let the guys know we're ready. They'll make sure that Vrex is right where he needs to be."

I'm really doing this. I'm really committing myself to a

fearsome warrior on an alien planet. And I can't wait to do it.

"Okay, then," I say. "Let's go."

We file into the small clearing next to the river and behind Rakiz and Nevada's tashiv. Mating ceremonies are usually held in the larger clearing in the communal camp space. But when we filled in Rakiz on my plan, he kindly offered up the smaller, more intimate area away from prying eyes.

Beth is waiting outside the tashiv, and she beams at me, dancing in place. "He's ready. We've got the chairs set up, and Rakiz is about to enter with Vrex from the opposite side."

"Awesome." I glance around, taking in the women who helped me put all this together. I wish Charlie were here to celebrate with us, but at least we know she's safe. "Thank you, you guys. I couldn't have done this without you."

Nevada grins. "Anytime. Now we're going to go sit down. Count to a hundred and then follow us."

They all hug me and then walk away, and I blow out a breath as I wait. And then I follow, walking around the side of the tashiv. I have a moment to take in the clearing, and my eyes sting as my mouth drops open. Alexis and Beth have decorated the area with flowers and lanterns, and all of the warriors Vrex is on friendly terms with are here, most of them grinning as I arrive.

And then all I see is Vrex as he appears, scowling at Rakiz as they walk toward us.

Rakiz nods at me with a smile, and Vrex turns, his mouth dropping open as his gaze finds mine.

He glances around at the clearing, and then he's stalking toward me, and tears roll down my cheeks at the look in his eyes.

Pure love.

He pulls me into his arms, and I smile up at him.

"So," I say around the lump in my throat. "I thought a quiet mating ceremony was more our style. What do you say?"

"I say that the gods must have mistakenly given me the happiness owed to a much better male. But I'm not giving it back."

I grin at him, and he brushes the tears off my cheeks.

"Is that a yes?"

"I'm afraid to close my eyes in case I might be dreaming."

I give him a pinch, and he laughs. Then he brushes my lips with his, and I get the full-body tingle I get whenever this man touches me.

He pulls me toward Rakiz, and I realize a fire has been lit. Ellie explained how the mating ceremony works, and I grin, taking the golden bands out of the pocket that Vivian arranged to be sewn into my dress.

Vrex freezes as he glances back at me, staring at the bands in my hand.

"You are more than I could have ever wished for," he says, his voice hoarse.

I grin at him. He doesn't know it yet, but we'll be leaving camp later today to honeymoon at his tashiv in the woods. While I love that he arranged for us to live at camp, we deserve some time alone.

I glance up at the green sky. Wherever Ilax is, I hope he can see how happy his friend is.

And I hope my dad can see how happy I am too.

The End

I hope you loved Protected by the Alien Warrior! I'm having so much fun with this series, and Charlie and her dragon are up next in Captured by the Alien Warrior!

The series isn't ending there though— there are at least two more books coming this year, including Zoey and Tagiz's story in Rescued by the Alien Warrior which is available for preorder now.

Want to be the first to know about freebies, new releases and sales? Sign up for my free newsletter here.

And don't forget to come say hi on Facebook- Hope Hart Author.

ALSO BY HOPE HART

The Arcav Alien Invasion Series

The Arcav King's Mate

The Arcav Commander's Human

The Arcav General's Woman

The Arcav Prince's Captive

A Very Arcav Christmas

The Arcav Captain's Queen

The Arcav Guard's Female

The Warriors of Agron Series

Taken by the Alien Warrior

Claimed by the Alien Warrior

Saved by the Alien Warrior

Seduced by the Alien Warrior

Protected by the Alien Warrior

Captured by the Alien Warrior

Rescued by the Alien Warrior

Enticed by the Alien Warrior

9 781959 293125